A motherless child. His grieving father. The cemetery where catastrophe comes calling once more . . .

His mother's death has left ten-year-old Nat with too many questions that have no answers — until he discovers her journal.

With the help of his new friend, Dee, Nat dodges his cemetery caretaker father and dives into the journal only to find himself facing an assault of hard truths about his mother's mental health that threaten to break him.

When Nat's world existence shatters into explosive grief, will it bring him and his father together, or will it only cause new wounds that are all the harder to heal — with Dee caught in the crossfire?

Everything We Never Knew is a suspenseful, heartfelt, and lyrically written story about grief, perfectly imperfect friendship and family, and the complications that can rise from a woman secretly struggling with mental illness, alone.

Content warning: eating disorders, miscarriage/babyloss

EVERYTHING WE NEVER KNEW

A NOVEL

ELIZABETH WILDER

CONTENTS

THE OOPS CLUB

FIND A TYPO OR GRAMMAR ERROR? LET ME
REWARD YOU FOR YOUR SKILLS!

Email the following to sheofthewild@gmail.com:

- Screenshot(s) with the error highlighted or circled
- Title of the book you found the error in
- Email you'd like your free ebook book delivered to
- Please use "Oops Club" as the email subject

If you're the first one to find the error, I'll send you one of my
ebooks books* of your choice — for free!

Thanks so much for supporting indie authors!

With love and gratitude,

Elizabeth

Anthologies, box sets, and collections excluded.

NAT

The boy sat on the edge of the grave, knobby ankles dangling one foot down into six, and wrote poetry.

Air and ash, he wrote, *air and ash are what I am, what anyone is.*

His father would be in the kitchen, making breakfast. The man only made breakfast on Sunday, after service. Every other day was either oatmeal on cold days or plain cereal on warm. *Blueberry pancakes aid the Sabbath rest,* he could be trusted to say over every batch.

His son wondered if the man believed the words, if he believed them himself. No one buried the dead on Sundays anymore.

His mother used to make Sunday breakfasts, too. He closed his eyes, phantom pumpkin waffles on his palate, doused in maple syrup. She'd never eat her own creations, though.

The boy opened his eyes, blinking hot tears. Air and ash.

A silvery wind of early fall tickled red and yellow leaves from balding tree limbs, sending them skipping through the cemetery, promising colder times to come.

He lifted his face, letting the slight crisp of the air cool his cheeks. Tomorrow he'd round up those scattering skeletons after school, but today was for rest and pancakes and poetry.

MIA'S JOURNAL

I wept when I found out that I am pregnant.

The closed toilet lid felt hot and hard beneath me in the clinic's ammonia-scented lavatory during yesterday's appointment.

I wept for the loss of me – I can never be just me, just Mia, again.

Now I am Mia plus baby, plus a child we didn't plan for, a child I do not want. Mia the progenitor. Mia the walking uterus. I've met my calling at last, my aunts will tell me, now that I've become a little mama.

Except I didn't ask for this uterus to go on procreating without my approval.

And then I wept for guilt, for my stinking, putrid shame. For my stupid and selfish heart. For Don, poor man, he didn't know what he married.

It had seemed so simple, so clear – he loved me, and I could love him. He courted me, chose flowers and built bouquets and poetry with such delicate and tender care, and worked and scraped and purchased white gold and the largest diamond he could manage and held his heart out to me with such a hopeful and tremulous little boy smile that I said yes and let him make me his wife. Forever, until death and all that.

And now, he's left me a microscopic love token in my belly as if it were just another flower, shoved inside me. He will probably be excited.

But then, he already rubs his callouses over my plush tummy and says it's sexy, it's hot, baby. He's either a liar or a fool or blind, or something of all three.

Or it's me, my strange brain. I wonder.

When the tears stopped, there in the clinic bathroom, I rubbed my cheeks against thin and scratchy toilet paper, washed my hands and face in the sink's lukewarm dribble, and pushed out the door, past the reception area, and out into the November morning, the distant smell of snow in the air.

3

DEE

It was cool at the bottom of the open, unoccupied grave. The early autumn's lingering humidity hadn't yet smothered the freshly turned soil. The girl sighed, the tiny whisper of content sounding muffled in the deep bed as she lay, eyes traveling the lines of the worn typeset of the library book, the dirt firm but just yielding enough along her spine.

She lay and read and let the cool brown of the dirt walls and the soft yellowing of the pages draw her deeper into the story, in and over and through words and worlds beyond what she thought of as the rather pale and paltry real one.

Her hand moved as if with its own thought, dirty-nailed fingers traveling between the flowered cotton of her skirt's pocket and her lips, transporting peanut butter laced chocolate. Her thumb and index finger were beginning to become sticky and brown, but only a little.

The candy still felt cool despite the noon's climbing temperature. She had left it in the freezer overnight so it emerged hard and cold in the morning, exactly as she liked it best, even in the frigid depths of winter.

She liked the candy's smoothness against the ridges of her mouth's roof, the pleasant density between her chewing molars, the salty sweetness. The treats seemed to bind her nearly twelve year old mind into raveling story, the levering of her hand a metronome for the words.

She would not, could not, have spoken any of this, told it to a listening human ear or scratched it into a secret notebook to be hidden away between mattress and boxspring until she packs up her life nearly another decade after to travel to higher learning. But that did not make it less true.

Beneath brown eyes, her cheeks rose full and flushed and lovely.

That was how the boy first found her.

NAT

He walked through the empty cemetery, letting the fingertips of his right hand trail along sun-warmed granite as he passed, opposite hand wrapped around a spiral notebook whose cover, once blue and pristine, was now scratched and dirty and tattooed with idle ballpoint pen sketches.

Anywhere else, the grass would have crunched beneath his sneakers, parched by the passing summer, but here it grew green and lush.

His father made sure of that. Visitors wouldn't be happy to see their dead blanketed by a brown and dessiccated lawn, although the boy wasn't sure it made all that much of a difference in the end. It was nice to lie down on, anyway.

Here and there the stone-marked landscape was interrupted by brown rises of soil paired with rectangular cutouts of earth, new-broken graves waiting to embrace gleaming coffins.

Visitors didn't like to go near the empty tombs, but Nat didn't mind, and thought the visitors didn't mind that he kept his distance, either. He would stare at their tears, the mournful expressions they hitched onto grim faces as they climbed from cars for a quick visit to the passed on.

He didn't understand what they wanted from standing over their departed, talking at the granite and marble as if the markers and the bodies that lay beneath could hear, as if they could care.

The empty graves were simpler, more honest. Perhaps that was why the visitors stayed away from them.

A scrap of color, almost earth brown but not quite, caught his eye's corner as he passed one of the yawning furrows.

A sparrow, he thought, *or a branch or leaves*, but even as he tried to convince himself of these possibilities, even before he turned to see the wisp of copper just in view on the floor of the grave, he knew it was none of them, that it was part of a human.

For the first time in his ten years, he felt afraid in his father's cemetery, in his home.

His heart pumped faster. He pinched his tongue between his teeth and peered over the earthy lip into the depths of the open grave.

A girl about his age lay there, pale cheeks almost translucent next to her auburn locks, lips an almost shocking pink, smudged with brown - dirt, he thought – reading a library-stickered paperback. He stared, skin prickling even in the clinging September heat, and loved her with all the confused feeling his heart could muster.

As the girl turned a page, she blinked and looked up, the boy's shadow falling across her face as she lowered the book, spine skyward, to her belly.

"Hello," she said, a smile in her voice before it reached her stained lips.

As quickly as it came, the warmth of love, of unasked for caring toward this strange girl with hair the color of flame, fled and the boy scowled, angry now at his previous flash of fear.

"What are you doing?" he said.

The smile dimmed but did not leave her face. "Reading."

He huffed. "*Here*, I mean."

Propping herself up on her elbows, she shrugged, book still carefully balanced across her abdomen. "Reading."

"In a cemetery?"

"It's quiet," she said. "And close to my house. It's too hot to go far."

He couldn't disagree. "You shouldn't be here," the boy said instead.

"Why not?"

"It's private. A — sanctuary." His father's word.

"Exactly," she said, raising an eyebrow at him. "That's why it's perfect. That's why I like it."

"I mean —" he paused, frustrated "— I mean that it's *private*. You're not supposed to be here unless you know someone. Unless you have someone here."

"Oh," she said. After a moment, she stood, dusting soil from the back of her skirt, particles still clinging to her curls. "Well. I'm Dee. Who are you?"

"I'm — well, I'm Nat," he replied, the words out of his mouth before he could register his surprise. "Nathaniel, that's my whole name. No one calls me that, though. Except my dad."

"Good to meet you." She grinned, waving up at him. "Can I stay now?"

"No," he said, shaking his head. "You can't."

She pouted for a moment, then shrugged. "Help me out, then," she said, reaching up a hand.

"Good thing you're tall," he muttered, tossing his notebook to the ground and lowering himself to the edge of the grave.

He took her palm, felt its stickiness as he pulled up, Dee bracing against his weight to walk up the grave wall. With some clumsy fumbling she emerged, and the two spilled out across the grass.

Nat was on his feet first. He looked down at the girl, hair even more brilliant in the sun's direct light, then down into the grave.

Dents pockmarked the soil walls that had previously been perfectly cut. He wondered for a moment, or maybe half a moment, if his father would notice, then shook his head.

Of course his father would notice, would see, would know and ask and add another sigh, another shake of his disap-pointed head to the pile he had already collected because of Nat.

It's a gift you've got, Nathaniel, he would say in a tired voice, *a real gift*. Only this time it wasn't Nat's fault.

"Thanks," the girl said from behind him. "I wasn't sure I could get out by myself."

He didn't turn, still staring into the empty tomb. "Then why did you go down there in the first place?"

"I don't know," she said after a moment. "It seemed like a good idea, I guess."

"Well, it wasn't."

"Hey," she said. "I'm sorry."

"It doesn't matter. Just look —" he started to point at the grave's walls, at the damage, into the future at the same tired talk from his father that was sure to follow that evening, then dropped his hand.

"What?" she asked, stepped to his side and trying to follow his gaze down. "What's wrong?"

"Nothing. You should go."

He could feel her hot stare on his cheek. "No. What is it?"

Nat turned, meeting her brown eyes with his own blue ones. "I told you. Nothing. Get out of here."

"You can't make me," she said, crossing her arms over her chest, pouting lips still smudged brown.

"Yes, I can. Leave."

"What, you own the place?"

"Yeah. So go. Before —" He was going to say before he called his father, or the police, or both — he hadn't quite decided — but it all sounded stupid even inside his head.

The boy hesitated for another moment, then turned, retrieved his notebook from where he had tossed it, and walked away, back toward the white house that crouched, petite and picturesque, beyond the mausoleum.

He could feel the girl's eyes between his shoulder blades for step after step, until finally he heard a shift, a tiny crinkle and, some moments after that, when he chanced a glance behind, she was gone.

Good, he thought. *That's good.*

The next morning, Dee was back.

He dreams of moon bugs and his mother.

The slivered, slimming moon peeks from clouds. The cemetery stands dark in the gloom, the shadows sticking to his footprints as if made of molasses.

Slow, step step step, he travels, the black mire thicker and thicker. But there, a glow beyond the night, whatever that means, he wants it, wants to feel it against his pebbly tongue, between his toes.

Arms reaching fingers claw, he swims and pulses against the bracken it is water now sludge swamping lungs eyes flooded bracken broken bracken the word in his brain like a drum's beat and nothing but sweat washed by muck mud mother — Mother — *he cries and chokes —*

MIA'S JOURNAL

I went to the bakery this morning and bought bread.

I love the tiny shop, with its old brick walls and ever-spotless glass — I don't know how the ancient Italian owners keep it so clean, I wish I knew their secret — arching over cases of russet loaves and rolls and cheerful legions of scones and croissants and cinnamon twists.

And the smell, warm and heavy with comfort, it makes me want to curl up in a corner and just rest, only waking to accept a proffered baguette, fresh birthed from the oven, dressed in thick purple jam.

But my favorite treat is not bread. Bread I can purchase without fear.

No, it is the square of sin, as I tell Ramona, the Italian woman who wears skin with folds as deep as the ocean and rises with a large and easy comfort. Peanut butter and chocolate chip together, my downfall.

She always laughs, a big laugh that seems to rumble from somewhere deeper or more distant than her belly, soft and ample from a lifetime of childrearing and pastry creation. I wonder, will that be me in forty years, round and bright-cheeked as I knead with flour-crusted knuckles whatever dough life brings to me?

She has beautiful hands, Ramona. Nails trimmed as close to the quick as she can manage, the luxury of long nails quickly becoming a nuisance, I imagine, what with dough and cooking powders and the like. Skin tanned from ethnicity and not the sun's crisping rays stretches over fleshy palms and fingers, not unpleasantly thick, but strong and soft and gentle when she pats my forearm and tries to press one of those damned peanut butter cookies into my own palm.

Most times I decline, politely, I hope, and place the treat back on the counter, feeling a bit guilty at the crumbs that crumble fall on the immaculate surface.

But sometimes I accept the gift and nibble, pretending to Ramona, to myself, that it will be okay, that the chocolate is not already traveling to my thighs, that I can't feel my body starting to swell with cellulite, that I'm not planning exactly how much extra exercise I will have to do to reverse the cookie's insidious effects.

And all the while, as these thoughts race each other through my brain in such hot succession that I barely can register one as distinct from the others, I am chewing, swallowing, tasting again, biting again, and even when I have finished, when it is finally gone I still want it, I want more and more and want the wanting to end and so I take my parcel of bread loves from the beautiful Ramona, Ramona of the fleshy arms and flabby belly, Ramona who is alight with some strange inner peace and love and joy in giving and serving and God knows what else, and I don't understand why I can see her beauty, why Ramona is the woman inside the body instead of the body around the woman, why I can't see myself, my own heart, the same way, why it is so damn hard to eat and live and breathe, why no one else can know this trouble.

And now, there is a baby, a baby that will swell this belly, and I'm supposed to feed it. Oh, help.

DON

The man stood at the tiny precipice's edge, staring down into the empty grave. He had noticed the marks on the grave walls, the hollows that traveled from the floor up and out of the rectangular space.

Not a squirrel or a bird, he figured. *Maybe a raccoon.*

But that didn't seem right either. It was almost as if something, or someone, had tiptoed its way up and out of the grave.

Even in the clear morning sunlight, the air not yet recovering its humidity from the respite of nighttime, the man shivered.

Although he had been in the business of death for the whole of his life, inheriting the cemetery from his father, who had inherited it in turn from his father's father, and so on back through long centuries and generations, he didn't much like to think of things coming out of graves, even empty ones.

He put people in their tombs, and they stayed there. That was the way of things.

No, the something that made these marks was very much alive, although he couldn't imagine what the marks belonged to.

He shook his graying head. It didn't matter. He had a funeral to manage in a couple of hours, and after that this grave would no longer stand empty and the marks wouldn't matter.

But he lingered there, frowning, his shadow leaping to lay on the floor of the grave, then up onto the opposite wall.

The man didn't like that the marks were there at all. He took special care to make each tomb he dug as clean and neat as possible. Out of respect, he thought, or maybe just habit. Whichever it was, he liked things to be tidy.

And this grave was not, not any longer. He'd have to clean it up before he set up the lift, before the mourners arrived.

Even as he turned away to gather the tools he'd need, some small restless part of his heart reminded him that they'd never notice the spilled dirt, never think twice about it, that he couldn't use them as an excuse, or as a good one, anyway.

NAT

The boy climbed the tree, gray bark pinching into his grasping palms. Grab, tighten, pull, a cadence for his arms while his stomach tightened, folded into itself, breath caught for a moment as his feet swung up before him, limp like a rag doll in that moment of suspension before muscles remembered their life, ankles reached and arched the bough and knees folded, embraced the purchase, and arms swung, grabbed, tightened . . . .

He perched, leafy hide-out masking him from view but allowing his own gaze passage.

The damp early fall lifted for a moment in the stirring of a breeze, almost cool, and he imagined that he is in a ship's crow's nest. He closed his eyes, heard wooden planks groaning, felt the rocking of the ship far below, the swing of the mast that seems small from deck is vast and pendulous in the lift.

That's what he called it in his mind, the lift. He leaned into the branches, enjoyed the hard knobs jutting into his back, the folded spiral notebook an uncomfortable comfort sand-wiched between bough and buttock, and he could believe that the limbs were lifting him higher into the summer blue.

He thought of his mother and wondered if she's watching him, gazing down from the beyond above. But then he real-ized, a tiny smile curling about his lips, that she had to be, her eyes guarding him a solid fact. He could be so stupid sometimes.

A *whirr-click-churn* rose from below, and it was not a tree sound, not an earth sound, not a sound of Monday morning peace and death and rest.

Reverie lifted.

He opened his eyes.

A figure at the foot of the tree, his tree.

"Hi." Dee waved up at him, one hand holding a camera spit-ting out snap shots onto the manicured grass, her finger still working the trigger. Lowering the black contraption, its long and well-used life apparent even from a distance, she smiled. "You looked so beautiful."

"Oh," he replied after a moment, not knowing what else he could say.

"Her name is Lucy," she said, nodding at the camera, now suspended from her neck on a strap.

He shifted, branches whispering around him. "Why Lucy?"

The girl thought for a moment. "I don't know," she shrugged. "I just like it. It makes me think of a very nice person."

"Who?"

She shook her head, red curls tendriling into ever-deeper tangles. "I mean that anyone who's called Lucy sounds like they should just be kind and good and lovely. That's the kind of person the name makes me think of."

"Even if it's a guy? A man named Lucy?" he called down, thinking. He couldn't conjure up a real person for the name, but liked the possibility.

What kind of a person is named Nat? he wondered. *Am I what someone would think of, or am I all wrong for the name? Or would that make the name wrong for me?*

She laughed, broad and full and from her belly. Nat couldn't help but smile back, and feel somehow pleased that he was responsible. He could make the red-haired girl laugh.

"I don't know. I guess maybe, if it's the right man. What a strange question."

The boy shrugged. "Maybe." He stared down at the camera. "What are you taking pictures of?"

Now it was Dee's turn to shrug. "I don't know. Anything. Everything. Anything that looks like it should be photographed." She slid a thick stack of exposed polaroids from her pocket, waving them up at him.

"Can I see?"

She pulled the photographs close in to her stomach, sucking on her bottom lip for a moment. The pictures she had just taken of Nat still lay scattered on the ground at her feet, like strange first flakes in a winter storm.

"Okay," she said, a small and sudden shyness hunching her shoulders a little. "If you want."

He shifted, leaving the sky behind as he clambered down the tree, jumping the last bit and landing on the grass with a soft grunt, careful not to crush any of the photographs between his sneakers and the dirt.

"Which do you want to see first?" she asked, still holding the pictures with tight knuckles.

Nat shook his head. "I don't know. Whatever ones you want, I guess."

She thought again, forehead creasing in a single vertical fold between her eyebrows. Then she nodded to herself and thumbed through the pile, pulling a few out. Without meeting his gaze, she held out the selected photographs.

"Here."

He accepted them gently, as if they were made of dried up leaf skeletons instead of plastic and paper and instant chemicals. Feeling the girl's eyes flicking from the photos to his face and back, he tried to ignore her nervous warmth beside him and take in the captured scenes.

Grass, huge and blurry, wildly green. A lit light bulb, the colors blown to near-white by its glow. A beagle, and then the beagle leading its owner away by the leash. Clouds and sky. And next, just sky, a square of cerulean, wide and crisp and bottomless even in the white boundaries of the Polaroid. A purple larkspur. An open book, words arching away from the foreground in a soft haze.

Nat felt as if he stood moments too late, or perhaps too early, to decipher a great mystery.

He passed the photos back to her, nodding, not sure what to say. "Those are good." And then, "Thanks. For letting me look."

The girl shrugged. "Thank you for looking at them."

Nat nodded again, shoving his hands deep into the pockets of his jeans. The photographs remaining on the ground scattered over the grass, fluttering in a rising breeze. He bent and collected them, Dee kneeling beside him to do the same.

As he made a careful pile of the pictures, the top image caught his gaze. It was of himself, but that wasn't what held his attention. There was something on his face, some expression he had never seen there before, perhaps because it was not the sort of thing you could see in a mirror.

In the photograph, he sat suspended in the tree's branches, eyes taking in nothing and everything. Sunlight broken by leafy shadows splotched his face, and one eye gleamed brighter than the other.

There wasn't really anything special that Nat could pick out – his sneakers were beaten and untying as always, brown hair mussed and in need of a trim. Even the photography itself seemed unremarkable, his frozen form a little too far away from the camera, the sun's rays flaring against the lens, the whole image smeared in a barely unfocused haze.

And yet, there was something.

"What is it?" Dee asked from his side. He blinked, first at the photo and then up at her, her presence almost forgotten in his reverie.

Nat looked back down at the photo resting on the top of the stack cradled in his palms. "This," he said, then stopped.

"Yeah?" she asked, the fingers of one hand tugging at a bunch of grass. "What about it?"

He shrugged. "It's . . . I don't know. It's just – good."

"Oh," she said, a half-smile lifting a corner of her raspberry colored lips. "Thanks. You looked so lovely up there. Peaceful, I guess. I didn't mean to bug you, though."

Peaceful, he thought. Maybe that was it, the mysterious attraction of the Polaroid.

"It's okay. You didn't bug me." He passed the rest of the photos back to her. Dee accepted them all except for the one that had so taken him in.

"No," she said, "you can keep that one."

"What am I going to do with a picture of myself?" he asked, staring at the proffered square.

"That's up to you," said the girl, waving the photograph at him with a shake of her copper hair. "I think it belongs to you anyway, so you should just take it."

So he did, and he felt a strange shift in his gut, a relaxing, and he realized he had been holding his stomach muscles taut and tight. *Maybe she's right*, he wondered, *maybe it's always been mine.*

He shook his head. "Thanks."

Dee nodded, grinning. "Sure."

They stood for a moment, the girl shuffling and sifting the photos in her palms, the boy staring at her, catching himself and looking away, only to find his gaze drifting back to her face.

"So," Nat said, finally, the word exploding from his throat, belying the awkward weight of pressing silence on his shoulders, his mind, his heart.

She looked up at him, lips curling into a sly smile. "So," she replied, squarely returning his gaze.

He pointed at the camera slung about her shoulder. "Do you take pictures a lot?"

"I guess," she said, finger the camera's strap that halved her cotton-printed chest. "I like to take pictures of things, if that's what you mean. I don't think about it much. I just do it."

The boy nodded, thinking of the notebook still folded and stuffed into his jeans' back pocket. He liked to write, he supposed, but sometimes the words just came, as if it wasn't him thinking them but something or someone else speaking to him, and he simply scribbled the words onto paper.

Or perhaps the words weren't spoken by anything at all, maybe they just existed all around, part of the earth and air and water, and sometimes he could hear them or read them or *feel* them brushing against his cheeks, against the back of his neck, and he just reached out with his nubbin of a pencil and pinned them to the page.

He thought that was what butterfly collecting must be like, borrowing a specimen of delicate rainbow light and coffining it in a tiny glass box.

He wondered if poetry was murder.

"What about you?" Dee asked.

The boy shook his head. "What about me?"

"What were you doing up in that tree?"

"Oh." He thought. There had been plans of writing in his mind, but they'd been vague at best. And there was the ship, letting the tree's swaying pass him out of this reality into a half-waking dream place that smelled of salt and fish and sodden timber.

But before that, his fist purpose in the climb. . . .

The grave. His father. Waiting and watching.

There it was.

"Well," he said, staring down at his dirty sneakers. "I was going to – I mean, I was trying watch, see what he was doing."

She frowned. "Who? What who was doing?"

"Sorry. My dad," he said.

"Why did you have to climb a tree to do that?" the girl asked.

"Because I don't — I didn't want to bother him," Nat finished lamely.

He had been going to say, *Because I didn't want him to see me,* but he didn't want to tell the girl that, to tell her how she and the mussed empty grave were the reason he was spying on his father in the first place. And he didn't quite know why he didn't want Dee to know that, to know of her error, her responsibility in the matter.

"Were you hiding from him?" she asked.

Nat stared. "No," he said, voice now loud.

Her brown eyes narrowed, top and bottom lashes brushing against one another as she searched his face. "I don't believe you. Why would you have to hide from your dad?"

"I told you, I wasn't hiding, I just didn't want to get in his way," Nat said, hands balling into fists. "He's really busy, there's a burial in a couple of hours—"

Dee's eyes grew huge now. "A burial? Can we go?"

"What?" He stared. "Are you crazy? Of course we can't go!"

"Not even if we dress all in black and pretend we know the person who died?"

Nat shook his head. "No way."

"No one would bother us, if we were quiet."

"*No*," he said. "No. Besides, my dad would see and I'd get into trouble."

"What if your dad didn't see you?" she asked. "Would you go with me then?"

"No. And you're not going either."

"Come on, it would be kind of cool. Plus I bet I could take some good pictures, if I was sneaky about it."

He took a step closer to her, breathing harder now. "No! You can't go, so stop talking about it. It's not allowed, and even if it was allowed that wouldn't make it okay. You can't just go around taking pictures at people's burials. It's – it's just wrong."

"Where's your mom?"

"And – what?" Nat felt his mouth dropping open as the bottom dropped out of his stomach.

"Your mom. Where is she?"

"I don't get it," he said slowly, wary.

"You haven't mentioned her. And I've only seen your dad."

"Well, where's *your* mom?" he shot back. "Or your dad, and your family? I mean, I don't even know where you come from."

"Good point," she said, nodding. "My mom's at home, which is down at the end of Harbour Terrace —" she pointed in the general direction "— and she's probably painting because that's what she does, she's an artist. My dad's a teacher, and we just moved here so he could teach English at the high school. And I haven't got any brothers or sisters, and my only aunt runs a school in Africa. We don't know about my dad's family because he grew up in orphanages and foster care. Oh, and I have a dog named Beckett."

"Ah," he said, blinking, taken aback by the flood of information. "Um, good to know."

"Your turn," said Dee, poking him in the shoulder. "Where's your mom?"

Nat scowled at the girl. "She's not here."

"Where is she?"

"She —" he took a deep breath, held it for a moment, and then let it rush out in an explosive stream. "She's just not here."

"Did she leave? I hear about that happening all the time. Did she run away with someone, to have another family? Or did—"

"Shut up," the boy found himself growling. "You *shut up*."

Dee stared for a moment, brow furrowed. "So that's it, then, isn't it?" she asked, voice whispery. "She left."

Without thinking about it, Nat stepped forward in one smooth motion and punched the girl in the jaw, sending her firey crop spinning, glinting in the sunlight as her head whipped around to one side.

And then he froze, every muscle taut as icy realization trickled down from his skull, past bruised pride and hot temper, his racing heart, curled and throbbing knuckles.

I hit a girl, he realized, the contents of his stomach churning as his gut clenched and soured. *I hit a girl. I hit* her.

He staggered back, widening the rift between her quivering form and himself, and at the same time he wanted to reach across, smooth her hair, mend the hurt. But he couldn't, because how could the hand that caused the pain be the same one to take it away?

"I—" he croaked, eyes still widened in shock at his own actions, "I'm —"

But before he could coax the apology from his choking esophagus, the girl turned back toward him and pummeled his shoulders with twin fists, a single hit on each side that sent him crashing down to the earth.

He lay there, stunned and angry and ashamed at his anger, the hot and cold emotions circling one another, circling his brain, in a circus of horrible and devouring phantoms, and she stepped over him, casting a shadow across his face as he stared up.

"Don't you ever touch me like that," she spit, voice ragged and hard.

Her slitted eyes, the brown barely visible, pierced him, a twisting knife in his spleen, her hurt and rage worse than the fact that a girl had knocked him down, almost worse even than the fact that he had tried to knock her down first, and failed.

But not worse than the fact that he had hit a girl.

This girl.

And then she was gone in a flutter of cotton, running away, away from him.

Nat did not move, but continued to lay there, staring up through the waving branches of the tree and the blue beyond. It didn't seem possible that the morning was still bright and cloudless, the tree not dead and withered in horror.

He spread his arms out from his body, feeling the firmness of the earth still the same as it ever was. The grass painted his palms with cool green kisses, and his laced his fingertips into them. And then he felt something that was not grass but felt hard and slick and clean-edged.

He turned his head and picked up the photograph, the Polaroid that she had taken of him, and he saw again how she had captured some indefinable part of himself that he had never before seen, and he wept.

8

MIA'S JOURNAL

Today I told people about the baby for the first time. People other than my husband, of course.

Don reacted exactly as I thought he would, and somehow differently, all at the same time.

"That's wonderful," he said to the news, folding me — no, us, now, us forever — into his arms. And then, pulling away but keeping my shoulders squeezed between his wide hands, "Are you all right, love?"

I looked at him. What could I say? I shrugged into his palms. "It's quite a surprise."

"That's not what I asked."

"There's a lot to be done. Doctor's appointments, new furniture, clothes, budgeting." I stared at the buttons traveling up the front of his plaid shirt. "We should probably read a book or something, learn how to be parents. How do you become a parent?" I glanced up to meet his gaze, warm and blue as ever, picking at one of his shirt buttons with a finger.

ELIZABETH WILDER

He shook his head. "I don't know," he said, shaking his head. "But we'll figure it out, I promise you. We will learn and change and be parents. Good ones. The best we are able."

"What if our best isn't good enough though?"

Don squeezed my shoulders. "You will be a fantastic mother. I know it. And you're not alone in this. You're never alone."

"I know. But God can't raise this child."

He paused, a frown stretching across his shaven chin. "I meant me, that I'm here, I can help. That I want to." Another pause. Then the question, again, "Are you all right, Mia?"

I nodded, biting at my tongue, willing the threatening tears to abate. "Of course," I said, voice trembling only a little. "Never better."

But later, while surrounded by the women of the church, some with their own young children, some without, and some old enough to be my own mother, a community of womanhood and breasts and uteruses, I was all right, really and truly.

Slender fingers, light with tenderness practiced on infant tears and rough with the scouring of legions of dishes and toilets and wrinkled and worn laundry, rubbed over my shoulders, brushed my hair, pressed into my wrists with real empathy, with the weight of having walked the path before, smoothed it into a safer passage with each generation, each bloody, unromantic birth.

hey knew, they knew the silent tears that stain my pillow at night, the clammy terror that shrouds my chest that I'm not ready for this, can never be ready for this.

There, in the quiet of God's house, in the care of women in their rose-colored fingernails and carnation-printed polyester dresses, I felt my breath rise in peace, fall out of my lungs with a calm not felt since the

30

clinic, since I learned of my passenger, my fetus, my baby. And it was all fine, so very fine that I could return their smiles with a real one, trembling in the knowing that I am mother.

I touch my belly, now, and place Don's sleeping hand on top of it and wonder.

9

NAT

The sounds of chewing were too loud in the boy's ears, filling the silent kitchen.

Nat enjoyed sounds, felt as if they were massaging into his brain, soft and pressing and filled with quiet and calm that made his muscles release, lulling him to an open-eyed reverie without the heavy gluten of sleep. The sound of a paintbrush dabbing color over a canvas, a movie detective's shoes as he pursued the killer's trail down a dark and rain-slicked alley, the soft cacophony of any syndicated cooking show, the mastication of cereal in his own mouth or any other. They worked into his scalp, these noises, through bone and fluid and cerebral flesh into the deep crannies of his brain, his mind, into wherever his soul was kept, and soothed him.

He sat with his father at the kitchen table, the glimmers of fading dusk filtering through windows to illuminate the counter of used dishes, leftovers growing cold still in their stove-top vessels, the partially eaten spaghetti and salad dinner disappearing from their plates in quiet consumption.

Squash squish, Nat heard the pasta say inside his mouth, almost a part of him, lingering for another few moments on the precipice of ownership as his jaw works before throat muscles convulse and grasp and pull the pale gob down into acidic absorption. And then another forkful, lettuce and cucumber, crackling into a fibrous mass against his mouth's roof.

"Good day, son?" His father's gravelly voice seemed loud in the still kitchen, and yet quiet over the boy's half-chewed greens.

"What?" he asked, pressing the vegetables into his cheek.

The man's right eyebrow jumped a centimeter, forking twining into tomato-soaked pasta strands. "What did you get up to today?"

"Um," said Nat, swallowing too soon and losing the meditation of mastication in a coughing fit. Gulping at his water cup, he spluttered until the tickling in his throat eased and the mishandled mouthful had tucked safely into his stomach. "Um," he said again, "not much, I guess."

"Don't you remember?"

He shrugged. Of course he remembered. How could he forget? The too-fresh, too-vivid memory of his knuckles slamming into Dee's soft cheek rushed into consciousness, and he felt as if she stood there in the kitchen and kicked him in the stomach in deserved retribution. "Just hung around. Wrote a bit."

"That's great," said his father, nodding. "How is the writing going? Going to publish that novel soon?" His small smile traveled across the sparsely set table to the boy, blue eyes not unkind.

Nat shook his head. "I'm not writing a novel, I told you."

The smile faded a bit, but the man nodded. "Right. My son, the poet. The next T.S. Eliot, maybe?"

The boy couldn't help the half-grin that spread over his lips. "That would be cool." T.S. Eliot was his dad's favorite poet. The older man had read Eliot's work to Nat since the boy's memory began, sometimes before bed or while relaxing in the evening after a particularly filling and just-too-comfortable meal. Or, Nat's favorite, on a stroll through the cemetery, entertaining the still and decomposing guests, as his father liked to say. Nat liked to think of the dead, slowly turning to dust, feeling the pair of footsteps traveling over their coffins, countless watertight homes until the end of time, muffled rhymes and iambs filtering through the soil.

His father speared a piece of broccoli, winking at the boy. "You're not wrong, there, not wrong at all. And maybe you'll even let me read some of your poems one day."

Without thought, Nat's free hand traveled to touch the beaten notebook that rested next to his plate. "I don't know," he said, pushing at his pasta with the fork in his other hand.

The man held up his hands as if in surrender. "There's no hurry," he said. "That day will come soon enough. But it will have to come at some point if you want to be more than another Emily Dickinson."

"Dad, she was a girl!" said Nat, wrinkling his nose.

"Okay, so you'll be a young, male, and extremely handsome Emily Dickinson. But you see what I'm getting at."

Nat nodded. He knew that poets these days had to not just write, they had to read. In front of other people, huge audiences, sometimes. Just the thought made his stomach churn, much to its partially-filled chagrin.

"What's this?" His father's broad hand flicked toward the notebook. Nat followed the motion with his eyes, saw a tiny white corner peeking out from beneath the scored cover. Frowning, he lifted the blue cover and sucked in his breath. It was the photograph that Dee had given him that morning, that he had spent the rest of the day fingering, remembering, before tucking it away at the front of the notebook and pouring out graphite tears and some salty ones over the spiraled pages.

"It's a photograph," the boy said, staring at the slightly hazy image. "One of those Polaroids."

"I can see that. Tell me about it?"

"It's me. In the picture, I mean."

"Where did you get it?"

Nat bit his lip for a moment. "A girl. She took it when I wasn't looking."

"May I?" His father held out his upturned palm, eyebrows lifting. The boy hesitated for a moment, then, his own hand feeling as if weights dangled from his bony wrist, passed the plastic square across the table.

The man sat gazing at the photo for long moments, strange shadows seeming to play across his time-grooved forehead. "Well," he said in a husky whisper, "well." A heavy pause. "This is quite something, isn't it." It was not a question, and Nat did not offer an answer. And hadn't he felt something like what he now saw in his father's blue eyes when he himself first looked at the picture? *At least I know I'm not crazy now*, he thought. *Unless it runs in the family.*

"You look —" His father choked a little, and Nat felt a stab of alarm in his gut at the tears that suddenly flooded his father's eyes. The man blinked and tightened his jaw. "A girl took this, you say?" he said, voice strained.

Nat nodded. "Yeah, she just showed up, and she had a camera. Her name is Dee," he added after a moment.

"Mmm," said his father, and beyond the unspilled tears there now gaped a too-familiar distance.

Nat sighed. The conversation was over, he knew from experience. But he was curious, and asked the question that itched at the forefront of his brain. "What do I look like, Dad?" he said, crossing his fingers. "In the picture? What were you going to say about what I look like?"

The man sat in stillness, staring into the tiny image as if willing it to speak some great and hidden truth to him, or the answer to an eternity or riddles, or a poem of love.

"Dad?" he said again, and slowly, the man shifted, almost imperceptibly, and the reverie broke.

"Nothing," the man said, voice now dull and heavy. "It was nothing." Reaching, he placed the photograph on top of the blue notebook, face down. Nat covered it with his own hand and put another bite of salad into his mouth and chewed, *crunch crush*, and waited for the sounded to work his consciousness into quiet stillness. But his mind wouldn't calm, and the kitchen, the sun now set and darkness pressing in all around, stood cold and silent about the two figures at the table.

The boy did not sleep that night. Or, if he did sleep, it was a churning half-rest, scalp sweaty and bothered against the pillow that would not yield to comfort, to even the most feverish of dreams. If he dozed, it was clammy and unpopulated. When he tossed in wakefulness, alternately kicking away and grabbing at twisting, snaring blankets, faces seemed to hover in the dim just out of reach.

Dee, cheek swollen and purple, brown eyes hot and angry. "Don't you ever touch me," she spat, "don't you ever touch me." Again and again, ugly voice hissing forth from the face his heart had loved and hated and then decided to claim as friend only to betray, the Judas of his fist his new master, twisting coppered curls into the snakes of Medusa with a venom and hunger for his soul. And it was hers for the taking, for he had ruined her, ruined their friendship, he knew, and that knowing was the worst for it lived in his gut, in his mind, and he could not take breath or let his lashes fall or feel the beating in his chest, the core of his small and paltry life, without feeling the blade of responsibility behind his ear, held by his own cold-fisted hand.

He imagined the specter of his father standing in the shadows, phantom of the man who the boy could hearing snoring in the next bedroom, blue eyes oozing pain and sticky hurt. *Why?* asked the mirage without moving its lips, words playing in the tossing boy's mind, *Why did you make me remember? I live to forget. I live to forget, and forget you, you wretched slip of a creature. Why won't you let me be? Let me die and live among the guests, they're so much kinder.* And next, his mother, smiling at her father and shaking her head, slower than the rasping crawl of the analog clock sitting on the nightstand, ticking away the ever-lengthening night.

"Mom," he croaked, lifting his too-heavy head from the bed. "Mommy."

She turned to him, raised a single finger to her rose-colored lips, halting his words, blonde head still shaking, *left right left right left* in a nauseating cadence and she glided forward, leaned over his prone form. And he closed his eyes, waiting her cool kiss to take seed on his forehead. But instead came a soft coarseness that blanketed his face and he reached up as it caught in his nostrils and he tasted cotton on his tongue, his palms feeling rectangular plush yielding and he could feel her hands on the top of the pillow, pushing down and down and down and he screamed into the fibers but they absorbed the sound so it came loud all around him but too soft in the room, the sleeping house, and long seconds passed into dizzy minutes and he spiraled deep into the earth and fell into the waiting casket, the guests applauding his arrival. *Right on time, boy,* they all whispered, *right on time.*

DON

The television lit the bedroom in restless phantom blues, ever-flickering shadows of late night reruns and culinary informercials across the master bedroom's walls. The man lay half-covered in the four poster bed, bedspread tangled about his legs. He clutched a pillow, cheek sinking into its softness, and imagined that it was the bosom of a woman, of his wife. Squeezing his eyes, burning with unspilled and long-fought tears, he tried to make the tapestry of the coverlet into her corduroy shirt, to will the rise and fall of a figment chest.

But the deception did not hold, never even sank the lightest illusion into his brain, not tonight. The man sighed, untwined his arms from around the pillow and rolled over.

He lay and considered the television remote that rested on the opposite nightstand. He should turn off the t.v., he knew, for perhaps then sleep would finally come, letting the churning of his brain grind to a sticking halt for a few hours. But then the darkness would bring shadows and silence for his ghosts to tuck into, circling the bed, unseen but felt in all their clammy jealousy, coveting his shirt, his skin, the blood and beat that counted him among the living. *Officially, anyway,* he thought.

But he did not stir, did not inch an arm or finger or fingernail toward the remote. The mute radioactive images, somehow benign and macabre at the same moment, stood sentinel over his night watch. Besides, the remote seemed so far away, such a long way to travel. The silent drone of the illuminated box was better.

Even as the thought passed into consciousness, as once more he embraced the restless quiet, a deep groaning filtered into the room. At first the man did not hear it, or if he did his brain dismissed it as a figment, as his own wishful or lofty or grief sick mind. Then it came again, muffled as if it had squeezed itself into being beneath a heavy rug or from the innards of a wall. And then again, and longer this time.

Don lifted his head from the pillow, eyes wide but not seeing, every spark of energy he could muster poured into the act of listening. And it seemed to require that much concentration, that much will, and he could feel his heart's pace quicken with the effort.

The room seemed full of the sound, low but almost without break or pause now. *This is it,* he thought, a chill shivering down his chest, *my time. The guests rise to claim me, take me home.* And then, in a flare of queasy hope, *She has come for me. At last. She's returned.*

But the groaning, no longer deep and long but rising, almost shrill with some new tang that Don placed after a moment, paired with the sharpness in his own gut. A whine, a shriek of fear, of releasing panic.

It felt like an explosion behind his eyes, shattering sparks and fiery ashes across the innards of his forehead, of his slow and stupid brain. And now the bed sheets, which had felt almost comforting just a moment ago in their serpentine hold over his ankles, coiled and strained against him as he flailed, tumbling from the mattress to the floor in a heap of joints and middle-aged aches and flurried curses.

Nat, he thought, the voice behind the moaning, the crying, now obviously belonging to his son, his *son* and he hadn't heard, hadn't recognized. What kind of a father was he, booze stupefied, she had been right, years and memories ago *how do you become a parent* and the damnable sheets but not damned because they had been hers, her choice, she picked them out at the department store and said they spoke of sleep and porcelain and Holland and sky to her and *Nat Nat Nat* like an automatic's report and *shit* finally free, palm on knob and feet *left right* down down the carpeted hall bathroom bathed orange from the night light like flames like fire *had she arrived* the house burned but no, just his own phantoms again again but the wailing true like breathing, like careful drowning, louder and quieter and —

"Nat!" he shouted, the night showering around him in shards as he let the name fly, banishing the darkness from his son's room as he shoved his palm up against the light switch plate. "*Nat*, what --?"

The words died as his eyes took in the sheets, as tangled as his own had been moments and eons and moments before. A pillow lay over his son's head, and the boy's torso writhed as if to be free of the plush burden even as his spindly arms crushed the mass down into his own face.

Don stood frozen, forehead crumpling in confusion. *The guests*, he thought, *they're here, but not for me. They've come for the rest of my heart, but they don't want my body still, cruel bastards.*

Another shriek and twitch from the bed and, guilt and fear stabbing at his belly, the man realized that his son was truly, horribly, smothering himself. He leapt forward, tore the pillow from eleven year old fingers, surprised at their thin strength.

Throwing the pillow to the floor, he bent over his son, who lay gasping. The boy's face shone crimson, slick with sweat, drenched hair mussed across his pillow-creased forehead. He still twitched and moaned, but the trilling screams subsided as soon as the pillow lifted.

"Nat," his father said, swallowing hard to find his voice, to shut the panic out of its sound. "*Nat.*"

The boy stirred, heading lolling a bit. His mouth worked soundlessly for a moment. And then, "Mom?"

The word, voiced in that dry and pathetic sigh, felt like class bursting inside Don's gut. He sat, immobile, staring at Nat as wakefulness slowly dawned on the boy, his own brain churning. *Was I right?* he wondered. *Was she here?* He rubbed a hand over his stubbly chin, exhausted.

Nat's eyelids flickered then rose, the whites of his eyes as red and chafed looking as his father's felt. The man pushed aside the phantoms who began had begun to rise and circle even in the safety of the overhead lights and ran his fingers through Nat's sweaty hair.

"Hey," Don said, gazing down at his son, searching the boy's strained face without quite knowing what he was looking for.

Nat swallowed once, twice. "Hi," he rasped back.

"You were dreaming." *I think*, the man added without voicing the words. *I hope.*

"Oh."

With a smooth motion he pushed the damp bangs back from his son's eyes, feeling the heat of the boy's skin from inches away. "You okay?" he asked after a moment.

The boy stared up, past the graying head bent over his own, unspoken monsters and nightmares playing at the back of his eyes. Don felt another pang in his heart, his belly. *How did I become a parent?* Blinking, Nat squirmed, shrugged a shoulder, the sheets bunching beneath his form.

"It was just a bad dream," his father said, nodding down at him with a small smile, wishing he could believe the words he tried to lie such confidence into. "That's all. It's gone, and when the sun comes up I bet you'll laugh at whatever it was."

"Mom . . ." whispered the boy, voice cracking, trailing away for a moment. "She was here. And you were, too, I think, and Dee." *Dee?* the man frowned. And then, recalling their dinner-time conversation, *The girl. Nat's new friend.*

"But definitely her," Nat was saying. "Mom." He met his father's gaze, bloodshot eyes full of questions the man could not discern, questions he couldn't answer even if he knew what the questions were.

"I dream about her, too, sometimes." Don wondered how much his son knew, if he suspected how his father spent his nights, numbed to eventual half-sleep, every night since he went to his bed alone.

"She was here, Dad. Right here. But —" the boy swallowed hard "— I don't think she was very happy. With me."

"It was just a dream," Don said again. "Sometimes our brains lie to us in our sleep. Don't you listen, don't you even think of that. Of course your mother was happy with you." *Of course*, the man thought. *Of course she was*. He wondered if he was lying to himself now, and if it mattered.

Nat shook his head. "Yeah. I know." His face seemed suddenly paler, and his chest shuddered with the force of a great yawn. "I know," he said again, the words sluggish, spoken through a morass of descending sleep. *The sleep of children*, Don thought in some detached crevice of his brain, *blessed and easy and easily stolen*. He wondered if he had read that somewhere.

The man retrieved the pillow from where he had thrown it. Lifting the boy's head, skull steel-strong and somehow so fragile in his own wide palm, he eased the pillow beneath it, let the boy's hair halo across it, Nat already halfway asleep. Freeing his son's legs from the twisted sheets, he smoothed the blankets over Nat's form, tucking them gently around his shoulders. He planted a prickly kiss on his son's smooth forehead, then turned to leave the room. Flicking off the light, Don waited at the door for the sudden plunge into darkness to resolve into dim shapes and the murky shadows they cast.

"Dad?" came the small voice, thick.

"Yes, Nat."

"Thanks."

The man sagged against the doorframe, passed a creased hand over his face. *How can I be so blessed and so burdened at the same time?* he wondered. "Good night, son," he managed at last. And then silently, not knowing why he didn't speak the words aloud, *I love you*.

Back down the hall, feet padding over carpet, past the bathroom, into the master bedroom where the television still piped mute lies to its master. *Master of the house*, he thought, and bit at the inside of his cheek.

He picked up the bedspread and blankets, remade the bed and slid between whiskey-scented cotton strata. The indigo screen raced along a show about cops and car chases and shattered prostitutes. The man lay back against tapestried pillows, tried to let dull sleep come filter in. But the flickering broadcast was not powerful enough a talisman to ensnare his phantoms this night. Stretching, back twinging a middle-aged complaint, he reached for the remote and clicked the screen to glowing black and let the demons come.

MIA'S JOURNAL

Book club night.

I'm not sure why I decided to participate. I do love to read, of course, but to read as a collective a book that I did not choose — The Sun Also Rises *by Hemingway — seems odd. A bit like school, or what I recall of it. (It's strange, isn't it? It doesn't feel like it's been five years since college — somehow those five years stretch long in the saying of the words, five years, but I feel young still yet I'm closer to thirty than I am to twenty.)*

But the book club. Yes, it's a strange thing. Perhaps it was in the asking. The church ladies, women my age or older or, in one rare instance, slightly younger, can be quite convincing in their telling of need, of need for you to be present.

"We're starting a new book in a couple of weeks," one of them told me a few weeks back, Edith Henry in all of her polyester-ed, oatmeal cookie wielding glory, leading a clan of pigtailed and shiny shoed daughters. "Hemingway. It's a bit out of our usual scope, I suppose, but we wanted to read one of the masters and thought Hemingway would not be a terrible choice. We'd really love to have you."

"Oh," I said, taken aback. Why in the world would they really love to have me? I feel like I've always disliked these women, every flip of their salon-perfect hair, the way they roll their eyes at the masculine foibles of their husbands, legs smoothed into hose that I find itchy, gut constricting, hot, oppressive. And now I find that these women, females I thought so false in their ultra displays of femininity, want me, crispy-cuticles, unmoisturized, frizzy-topped me. How odd.

And it's quite tempting to suspect that I'm not much more than a fix-up project. Or that now that I'm a life-giver, life-bearer, I'm part of a new club and worthy of their attention, their friendship. But then I realize that even if that is true, some part of me that now speaks louder than my pride, than my degree-carrying, modern-mannered emancipated feminist tendencies, and I don't much care. Perhaps it's the microscopic force materializing in my uterus, or perhaps I'm just lonely for women. Who would have guessed that this could ever be true, for me? Ridiculous, really.

So tonight. Book club night, the first. I've read the opening section of Hemingway, like it as much as anything I've ever liked by him. And now all that remains is the gauntlet of women. Will I pass their test, or my own?

NAT

The pastor read from the letter to the people of Philippi. Nat closed his eyes and tried to imagine what it would have been like to be among the Philippians when the apostle's letter was read aloud among the congregation. Or perhaps the correspondence, written in another hand than its dictator, was passed from house to hearth around the new-believing community, parchment houseguest of welcomed, needed encouragement.

An elbow nudged into his ribs and he blinked his eyes open, once, twice against the sanctuary's light. At his side, the boy's father sat looking down at him, eyebrows raised and eyes a fusion of concern and reprimand.

"Sorry," Nat mouthed the word soundlessly with a shrug, opening his mouth more than he needed to be sure his meaning would be taken. The man nodded, the corners of his lips twitching downward a little as his gaze settled on the preacher once more, the hairy backs of his hands folded as if in prayer around the church's paper bulletin. Nat sat up straighter in his seat and did the same, stealing glances around the rise of Sunday-smoothed heads to see if anyone else had noticed, and was relieved that everyone was staring at the pastor and not at him.

"'Above all,'" read the pastor, brown-backed book balanced with years of practice in his outstretched palm, "*above all,* you must live as citizens of heaven, conducting yourselves in a manner worthy of the Good News about Christ.'"

A manner worthy, thought Nat. *Is that me? Do I live in a manner worthy of Jesus?* Probably not. His eyes trailed to the walls, painted pale peach, the color no doubt chosen by the pastor's wife, who never failed to bake something either peach flavored or colored for every church gathering or fundraiser.

At the front of the sanctuary to the side of where the preacher paced in exhortation hung a modest crucifix burdened with the artistically beaten and sagging form of Christ. Even from where he sat, Nat could see the painted crimson trailing from beneath his drenched crown, the utter exhaustion that made the Savior's ashen cheeks sag from his lolling head, the starkness of his ribs protruding from about his oxygen-deprived lungs.

For a moment, the boy imagined he could see the dying body shudder and arch, gasping for breath, longing for the end of life, of the battle for souls, of the temptation to abandon the post and regain the glory that none had the power or right to deny was his. But that's not what the Son of God and, somehow and simultaneously, of Man did, not by a long shot. Nat had already read ahead on the sheet of notes that came tucked in his bulletin: "When he appeared in human form, he humbled himself in obedience to God and died."

And died. The words tumbled about inside Nat's brain. *And died. And died and died and died died died.* He wondered if that's

49

what it meant to live worthy of Christ, as the pastor said, of the slumped and humiliated form, sweat and spit splattered, spit from his own people, people God had formed and loved and walked with.

The preacher was reading again, a verse that Nat did not see on the sheet of notes. "'Be humble, thinking of others as better than yourselves,'" the man said, head nodding above his crisply knotted tie.

Nat considered this, biting his lip. Did he put his father before himself? He didn't know, because he didn't know what that would look like. And he didn't have any friends, really, to put ahead or behind. Nobody wanted to be friends with the weird kid from the graveyard. *So I guess that one doesn't count for me,* the boy decided, shrugging a little to himself, collared shirt stiffly beneath the motion.

But his eye caught the form on the cross again, and again Nat imagined just that the human rendering of the Savior really did hoist his skull to meet the boy's gaze with one of such hurt and betrayal and pleading.

Is that the truth? the man-made Jesus seemed to ask, *The whole truth as you know it in your heart?*

Nat swallowed and knew that it was not. Because there was Dee.

He had not seen her since her likeness appeared in his room, and, as the boy was not sure that counted, he decided that he hadn't been seen *by* her since . . . heat swooped through his belly, and he shifted in his seated, swallowing at the sudden queasiness that oozed through his abdomen. Glancing up at his father, who sat perfectly still listening to the sermon, he wondered what the older man would think if he knew. Would he despise Nat, as the boy did himself? Or, worse, would he not care in the slightest? It could be easy, the latter. *He's never even seen her face*, thought Nat. But at the same time, perhaps that would make the former easiest. *Maybe it's easier to put others first when they're never around.* He shook his head, fingers mindlessly shredding the corner of his bulletin.

"'Fix your thoughts on what is true, and honorable, and right,'" read the pastor, the congregation seeming to heave and shift around Nat as if they as one entity sensed the imminent dismissal of service into a time of hand-shaking and fellowship and oatmeal cookies and coffee, "'and pure, and lovely, and admirable. Keep putting into practice all you learned.'" Even his father cleared his throat in the just the way he always did when closing an argument or sending the boy to bed. Everyone seemed eager for the pastor to bow his spotlit head in prayer and cue the worship band for a final refrain before sending the people on their way, to live the lessons he had so carefully pieced together that previous week, or not.

But Nat stared intently at the man, still reading the epistle writer's words into life, words whose span of two centuries both served to hold the boy enspelled in their vastness and by how cleanly they cut into his core. *"Putting into practice,"* he thought, and stuck out his chin in resolve.

When the final notes of the service's closing song vibrated over the congregation, Nat pushed through the crowded aisle and stood by the propped main doors, nearly hopping with anticipation. It felt like an age before he glimpsed his father's salt and pepper crop through tangle of clasped hands and cacophony of voices. Rolling his hands into tight fists and squeezing until he felt them throb with the lack of blood flow, then sticking them out straight, pointing like ten arrows set to fly down through worms and earth, bound for hell like the righteous spears of Jonathan, King David's cherished friend.

Except that Nat did not feel particularly righteous or cherished – or deserving of any such love or care – at the moment. But he felt the bite and binding of determination's fire, and that in turn made his breath come a little easier. *I can't take it back*, the boy told himself, *not ever. But I can make it better, maybe.*

It became a sort of cadence in his brain as he stood, swaying, fingers working and stretching and rolling. *Better, maybe maybe make it better, maybe.* He prayed, biting his bottom lip, that it was true.

"There you are," said his father, forehead creased as he approached the boy.

"Can we go?" asked Nat, forcing himself to stand still, fingers in twin balls now. "Can we leave?"

"I suppose. You don't want any cookies, don't want to say hello to Mrs. Greyson?" Mrs. Greyson was their closest neighbor, if cemeteries had neighbors and neighborhoods at all, and was the seemingly ancient survivor of seventeen cats, one trapeze artist turned railroad conductor of unknown and rather shady origins, and one husband.

No, thought Nat, *I don't want to hear about Mrs. Greyson's precious cats. Definitely not a good time for cat talk. Although the conductor story is a good one.* But even airborne train operators held no interest for Nat at the moment. His brain was spilling over with thoughts of *her*, of Dee, of making it better, just maybe, just maybe.

The boy shook his head. "No, I just want to get out of here."

The creases on his father's face deepened, and Nat wondered for the first time that day what his father thought about the previous night's blurry events, and wondered that he was only just wondering now. He shook his head, feeling all of a sudden rather muddled.

"What's the rush?" Don asked. And then, as if reading his son's mind, "I know Mrs. Greyson's cat stories can get a little out of hand sometimes, but she's a nice lady and it makes her happy that you listen, I think."

"It's —" started Nat, and then hesitated, words and lack of words catching in his throat. He shrugged one shoulder. "I guess I just don't feel like cookies. That's all."

The man stood, the chatter and easy hustle of post-service fellowship flowing around the pair, purple-shadowed eyes considering Nat. The boy tried to arrange his face into an expression of ease, of the faint uncaring of weekend leisure. He hoped he presented a fair imitation of whatever his father was searching for.

After a long moment, Don sighed and nodded, passing a palm over his shaven cheek. "We can go, then, it's fine. I suppose I could use a bit of a nap before putting things in order for tomorrow." Two burials were scheduled for the next day, one in the morning and the other in the late afternoon.

"Thanks," said Nat, and followed his father out of the church to where their sedan sat waiting in the dusty parking lot, the nearly midday sun already pricking sweat to life beneath Nat's collared shirt. Sliding into the car, Nat focused so strongly on Dee, on the mending of things, that it almost felt as if she was a physical presence in the car with them, sitting in the back seat. *I have to fix this,* he told himself, clenching his jaw. *At least I've got to try.*

When they arrived back home, serene and silent but for the occasional drone of a bumble bee, Nat launched from the car, slamming the door behind him so that the entire vehicle shook. And then, standing still and straight, he realized he did not know what to do.

Where did she say she lives? he thought, frowning as he tried to strain a street name from his memory. It was close by, he knew, close enough to walk to, that's why she had come to the cemetery in the first place. But that was all he could coax from his brain, still sluggish after the previous night, his own act of horror.

He stood next to the car, alone in the driveway. His father had already disappeared into the house, and would no doubt have already begun preparation for tomorrow's events. The wide expanse of the graveyard spread away before the boy, land sculpted smooth to meet with cerulean atmosphere in a steady, predictable embrace. Gray stones swelled and fell away across the earth.

Green blades yielded to Sunday best shoes as Nat wandered away from the car into the familiar granite crowd. With a sigh, he lowered himself to the ground, leaning against the headstone of one Vernon D. Miller, expired now for just about three years, beloved husband and father and all that. The boy pulled at the grass, heart a heavy weight on his stomach. *What can I do?* he thought. *What can I do now?* He glanced over his shoulder at the engraved granite, but Vernon offered no suggestions.

He sprang to his feet once more. *I can't just sit, I can at least try.* So he set off across the cemetery, past familiar gray shapes, past the now-occupied grave where he had first met Dee, the tree where he had hurt her, dirtied himself. *Try try try* his brain chanted with each footfall. All he could do.

A step on white concrete, skip-hop down the yellow-painted curb and he left the cemetery, legs taking the asphalt in wide strides. The boy's eyes swept the neighborhood like the lantern at the top of a lighthouse, searching for any sign of Dee even while he wondered what form such a sign or signal might take.

In the distance, far ahead of him just where the street curved into view from around a tree-dense corner, a figure walked on the opposite side of the road. He imagined wished prayed that it was her, gave the form a copper crown. A rehearsal played through his mind almost without his realization.

Dee, he would say, *I'm sorry. So sorry. I hurt you, and I'm terrible and if you never talk to me or look at me again I'll understand, really, but I* am *sorry, even if that doesn't make it go away, make it right. Are you okay?* He shook his head, omitted the question from the conversation. Of course she would not be okay. *Can we be okay?* And she would stare, eyes still angry, cloudy with uncertainty. Arms crossed across her chest, strong and tall-standing, she would finally finally dip her chin into those shining locks that pooled beneath her shoulders. *We can be okay,* she would say, *although that might not happen right away. Forgiveness is a long road to walk, or didn't you know?* He didn't understand her words, even as he knew they were of his own creation, but he would accept that, heart heavy but still beating, still living, folding her words, her reticent promise into its chambers always filling emptying filling again. He nodded at her in acceptance, acquiescence, obeisance and she waved at him.

The boy frowned as he walked in reverie. That didn't seem right. She shouldn't, wouldn't, wave, that much he knew. But the figure, the figure approaching on the street that shimmered waves of absorbed heat, the figure he had made into the girl, waved. He blinked, willed himself to see its true form and not the glamour he had laid upon it. But still it waved, and then Nat saw that the it was a she, and then he saw that it was *her*.

"Nat!" Dee called as she drew near, quick footsteps close to a run now. "Nat!"

He felt his arm rise from his side of its own accord, fingers stretched wide to receive and return her greeting. "Unh," he managed, and his feet flip-flopped to a halt and she stood there, reached out, pushed him gently in the shoulder, hair frizzy and full in the summer damp.

"Hi," she said, cheeks flushed, and the greeting sounded a little windstruck. Her brown eyes, trained on him, did not seem quite so full of hurt and hate as he had imagined.

"Erm." The words that had sounded so perfect, that flowed so easily through his brain in preparation just moments ago dammed somewhere between his memory and his desiccated esophagus.

"So," said the girl, tugging at a copper coil.

He nodded, wishing he had scratched thoughts of apology to paper, into iambic life. But there was nothing for it now. "So," he echoed, swallowing so hard that if felt like his was trying to unearth breath and saliva from some deep hidden place inside himself. "I —"

"I've been looking for you," the girl blurted out. "But you weren't outside last night, and I didn't know if I should knock on the door or not, if your dad would mind, so I didn't. And then I couldn't sleep because I felt so bad, so bad that I almost *did* go and knock on your door but then that made me feel even worse because I'd be stealing your sleep, so I waited until the morning, this morning, and then you were gone and your car was gone and I'm so sorry!"

He stared at her. "*You're* sorry? For what?"

"Well, because I knocked you down," said Dee, wrinkling her nose as if the reason was perfectly obvious.

"But *I'm* the one who should be sorry -- I mean, I am sorry. I -- I *hit* you. I hurt a girl." He stared down at his offending fist and wanted to wrest it from his wrist and toss it away he felt so sick with it, with himself.

"You did," she admitted. "You hit me, and that's not good, but not because I'm a girl. It would still be bad if I was a boy. And I hit you back, which makes me just as awful."

"I don't think you're awful," he muttered, not sure if he trusted her words to be real, and if he believed them even if they proved to be solid, to not be phantom letters drawn from over-thought fantasy.

"Well, I don't think you are, either," she said, jutting her chin out.

"Okay." He didn't know what else to say.

She shrugged. "Are we still friends?"

"I guess. Were we friends before?"

"Does it matter?"

He considered, a slow smile stealing across his face in spite of the continuing heaviness in his heart. "I don't know. I don't think so."

"Then let's be friends, okay?"

The smile became a grin. "I can be okay with that. Apology accepted."

"Just remember who apologized first," she said. "And if you hit me again, we're through."

Then she stuck out her tongue, and his heart swelled and swelled and he couldn't help but laugh out loud, rich and bubbling up from his gut, so hearty that he nearly wept.

13

MIA'S JOURNAL

I feel huge. And not just because I have this life growing inside me, swelling my gut in grotesque distention. It makes me shudder to touch my abdomen, when I glimpse myself sidelong in a mirror or window reflection, when I bend and must bend around the mass, when I feel the heavy tautness always pulling there. It makes me ill, or very nearly, and then I wish to be rid of this second life. I never asked for it. And then my illness multiplies because I have made myself sick in the wishing for an innocent's — the innocent's — end.

But today is a special hugeness. Book club, as always. It has become — or had been, until tonight — a special haven for me. Even when the discussion spins around a mediocre paperback purchased from the grocery store rack, I find myself nestling into the gentle whirl of female words and worlds as if into the cheerful heat emanating from a kindled fireplace during a winter's storm. Trading stories of children, of pregnancy (this, I suspect, largely for my benefit), of husbands' foibles to the accompaniment of fresh-brewed tea and honey. It is foreign in its beauty, this simple loveliness.

Until tonight. Eleanor, the hostess, brought out the usual steaming mugs and shortbread, crumbling and warm. But then, with a wink at me, of all people, she produced seeming vats of ice cream and a spread of sweet and savory trimmings. And she dug boulder-sized heaps of the frozen cream and sent them tumbling into a bowl, just for me, she said, and began to layer it with peanuts and chocolate chips and rainbow jimmies and warmed caramel. I watched in trepidation, all the while feeling the weight of my belly and wishing I couldn't feel it all, wishing I could be anywhere else.

If given another moment, perhaps I would have escaped on the premise of pregnancy sickness, of pregnancy fatigue, but I waited too long and the suddenly this mountain of fat and sugar and dairy rested in my palms and, as the other women helped themselves, I raised the spoon to my lips and slid a mouthful, heavenly in its horror, onto my tongue, down my throat, and dipped my spoon again, again, until the bowl stood empty but for a milky residue sliding about its bottom and I wanted to vomit, to rid myself of the added heaviness but could not, not there in another woman's house. So I sat and sipped tea and feigned absorption in a discussion that I can now remember none of as I sit here on the bathroom floor, leaning against the toilet that smells newly of vomit, the needing to expel my stomach's dwindling contents on the rise. And the life, the life that dwells so close in my belly, I wonder what it thinks, if it feels my thoughts, my disgust, if it hurts and how much more hurt is necessary to bring the tiny heartbeat to an end.

1 4

DON

The man waited in the kitchen for the cadaver and its entourage to arrive, reading. One of her books, and that's why he picked it. He'd never read it, a book Plath and all he knew was that the author was better at poetry or so they said. Or at least, that's what they, whoever *they* happened to be, knew her best for. And then she died with her head in an oven, so who knew what she would have been better at if she had lived as long as she should have. Unless she was always meant to bake herself out of this plane that must have done her such lonely and lovely hurt.

But he didn't believe that, didn't believe that anyone was meant to steal their own lives. Who did they think they were, to make such decisions? And besides, it all came down to cowardice in the end.

They had no mettle, he decided once. A father and mother had come to him, back when he first took over the place full-time, and asked him to attend to their dead daughter's remains. *Make her pretty*, the mother whispered. *Make her like she used to be.* The girl had locked herself into a car and lit up a pack of matches and let the whole rig burn. The police found her keys on the charred asphalt of the abandoned lot just outside the car, or what was left of the next morning, black-ened and malformed. Don wondered what was wrong with the woman, if she was stupid or if someone lied to her, to her husband, about what happened. In the end, he decided that the best he could do was a closed casket, propping a photo of the girl on an easel for the mourners to drip salty at.

And at the wake -- that was when he still attended the wakes instead of merely dropping the deceased off with the parlor staff and going to grab a cup of the blackest coffee he could find -- a friend of a friend told him that it had been about a boy. *A boy*, someone who may or may not have even known her, much less understood what she felt in the darkest and most secret crevice behind her beating heart, what she tried to convey those rare times she drew up her breath and nerve and unlocked that hidden place and let her weakness flow. A boy. He recalled shaking his head and muttering to himself as the friend of a friend wandered away to shed tears with a more empathetic companion, *That stupid, selfish bitch.* That was when he still cursed, and he smoked a little, too, so Don left the wake and went to fill his lungs and nicotine's smooth balm. He couldn't remember if the cigarettes helped that day.

Don found himself enjoying the Plath novel. In the short span of a mug of coffee and a bowl of grapes ingested at leisure, glowing supernatural green as the Monday morning sun shone through the clustered ovals, he read nearly eighty pages without feeling the drag of time passing or attention dragging, straining away. No, the typed ribbons of letters still pulled him in, made him want to crawl between their black print, to wander the streets and hotels of wealthy New York City, in what he imag-ined a more genteel time until he read of the exploits of Esther, the protagonist, chosen or otherwise, and even while he cringed at hers rooom mate and at the steady and winding *tick tick tick* of Esther's hypnotic psychosis, he turned the next page and the next and the chapters flowed by as he sat and waited.

That wasn't why he had selected the book to read from the modest wooden bookcase that uncomplainingly built its collection of dust in a corner of his bedroom. He loved to read but had trouble finding stories that suited him, and he didn't expect this particular paperback to meet with more success than any of the others he had tried, tasting a handful of pages or chapters before exchanging them at the used bookstore and returning home with a new armload of previously-paged words, eager to discover new worlds and characters molded from their authors synapses and sweaty predilections even as he dreaded the empty pages he would inevitably discover, the words moldy against his palate.

This book he did not count among those others, at least not any longer. He read on and spun deeper into the web of plot and motion and poet-spun literature and something inside him felt fed, satisfied. And as he turned each page, running his fingers over the rough leaves that had begun to yellow and turn brittle, he felt as if he read along with *her*, with Mia peering over his shoulder, her arms looped around his waist, kissing him on the shoulder to signal when she had finished the page and he would smile and his fingers find the next page with a rustle and they'd read on and on. He cradled the book's spine in his palm, leveraging it open with his thumb, knowing that her fingers, strong-veined and rough from dishes and all-over sexy, his wife's fingers had balanced the same spine, brushed over the same black print, thumbed at the same corners that still were folded into miniscule dog ears here and there. A lump formed in his throat as he thought and forced himself not to think of her and read on and on.

And by the end of the book, his cup of black coffee grew bitter and cold in the silent kitchen, not noticing how late his clients were running, he wondered if suicide really was all that cowardly, or if it was the best kind of love a desperate soul could manage to muster in the midst of a world of grief.

15

NAT

Nat kept his favorite photograph taped inside the front cover of his blue notebook. He had tacked it inside the first notebook he ever owned, the first notebook he ever wrote his own words and stories and poems in. His father had accidentally purchased an extra notebook at the start of the school year when Nat was eight years old, so he told the boy to do as he liked with the spare, or to save it for next year.

The possibility of the notebook, of the seemingly vast Siberian expanses waiting for him to press graphite into, to draw or scrawl life into penciled life. He liked the emptiness, the clamping of his gut muscles at the unfilled paper, a little afraid at the imagining, and afraid of not imagining. It thrilled him, made the hair on his arms prickle as he wrote and glued together great clanking poem-stories that felt too large in his mouth when he read them to his father. But his father would always grin and tell him to go and write, go and keep on being the genius of the family. So Nat would write more.

And slowly, slow as the gray cycle of January to February to March, spitting sleet and chills to penetrate the warmest sweater until it feels that May and June will never come, could never have existed — as slow as that, the words, his words, began to fit together like they were meant to, like they felt when his brain excavated them from the universe, turned them about and tried to birth them to the page unaltered. Only it never seemed to work like that, to transfer just right. But the words got better, easier, harder, and he kept his favorite photograph taped into the cover of every new book he ever started to capture his flow of words.

The photograph held two figures, facing away from the camera. One, very small and dressed in black pants and a crisp white shirt, was himself. Nat supposed that they must have just come from church or something because his mother was also dressed up, a red cotton sundress wrapping about her as she knelt at the side of the tiny Nat in the photo, pointing at something across the gray lake they stood on the shore of. Houses waited on the opposite shore, reflected almost perfectly in the water's surface. Sometimes Nat wondered what she was pointing at, what the photo version of himself thought of it. He couldn't see anything particularly interesting in the picture, but he didn't know that his current opinion mattered. When people were that small, even stupid, silly things were important, worthy of careful observation and study.

But mostly he just liked to look at this mother, at the way her curly blonde hair swept carefully but casually up into a knot on her head, little golden wisps flying away in a whisper of a breeze. He liked how he both could and could not see all of both their faces. How his mother leaned in close to his image to pass on knowledge and love that was for him alone, if only he could remember it.

He had even written a poem about it, although he didn't tape that into anything. He let that it stay where he had created the thing, tucked into the depths of one of his filled notebooks, stacked carefully in an old milk crate in his closet.

Crimson cotton brushes

white and we gaze,

you and I, across

the shining deep. You crossed,

pointing to the path

and left me, lonely

in your wake.

His father had suggested "wake" after Nat read him the first version, grappling for jus the right word, but the rest of the poem was his own creation in total. He liked it, although the boy also thought he could do better, that he had done better, but it really wasn't half bad. What he didn't like was how his father's eyes had grown red and swollen as he read, his voice thin and strangled.

"That's some lovely poetry, son," his father rasped and rose from the kitchen table where the two sat, brushing Nat's hair with his fingers as he left the room. He hated seeing his father cry, or just about to cry. The boy had only seem his father cry real tears once, three months before, tears that made the man wheeze and hyperventilate and finally crumple over the too-still form in the casket, blonde hair beautifully tended even in death.

Nat read the poem to Dee now, in the lengthening Sunday afternoon shade along the side of his house. Or really, he recited it from memory, and he was happy to see that it did not make her cry.

She clapped her hands, and he dipped in a miniature bow before throwing himself to lie on the ground next to where she sat. "That was great!" she said. "You wrote that for real?"

He nodded. "Yeah." He'd already shown her the photograph, who had inspected it closely, fingers hovering around the slick surface without ever marking them with an errant print.

"Well, it's really good. Fantastic, actually."

"Thanks," he said, feeling his cheeks warm. "I don't think it's fantastic, though. But thanks."

"I still think it's fantastic, and quite possibly amazing," she said, sticking out a raspberry-colored tongue. "Got any more?"

He stared for a moment. "Poems?"

"No, camels. Of course poems!"

"Oh." The boy looked down at the old notebook, open on the grass to the photograph poem. "I don't know."

Dee pouted. "What do you mean, you don't know? What's there to know?"

He shrugged a shoulder. "I don't know," he said again. "Nothing else is really finished. It's not ready."

"It doesn't have to be ready."

"Maybe. But I'd kind of like them to be before I go around reading them and showing them to people."

"First of all, I'm not 'people,' I'm just me," said the girl, raising en eyebrow at him. "Besides, have you ever gotten any of your other poems 'ready'?"

He thought, than slowly shook his head. "Not really."

"Then maybe I can help with that," she said, nodding her head. "If you want help."

"Help would be good," he said. *It definitely couldn't hurt*, he thought.

"Excellent. Now let's hear some more?"

"Right *now*?" He tugged at some grass. He'd never read more than one or two poems at a time, and only ever to his father. Something inside his stomach fluttered. It would have tickled if it hadn't made him feel quite so queasy.

"Don't wimp out," she said. "It'll be good for you, and for your writing. I mean, don't the great poets have to read their stuff all the time? They've got to have people to help them get ready. Don't you think they'd need that?"

He shook his head. Nat didn't know much about the great poets. "I heard that Shakespeare stole all of his ideas for plays," he offered.

"I bet he still had to edit and practice."

Nat sighed. "Fine, we can do this. I mean, I accept, your offer is accepted. But can't we wait a little? Let me at least pick some stuff that I want to make better, and then you can help. Okay?"

She stared at him, eyes roving across his face as if to discern some scrap of deception. Finally, she nodded. "Okay. But don't think I'll forget."

Nat smiled and swallowed, trying to ignore the flapping nausea in his belly. He had never realized how scary sharing his words could be. And, even worse, he didn't know why such a simple thing should be so frightening. *I wonder if it's normal.* He didn't know what to hope for.

16

MIA'S JOURNAL

I've left the Hemingway. It wasn't something I thought about, premeditated, it just was, is now. At the used book shop, trawling through the stacks of discarded spines, some so cracked and brittle you can barely read the title, others seeming brand new, I discovered a novel by a poet.

The rain drove me into the shop in the first place. It seems a bit late for this kind of rain, October weather misplaced in February -- clouds lumbering low and gray overhead, churning about each other in duel or dance, I can never decide which. The morning rolls into afternoon and still the great mountains of vapor hold back, refuse to share the contents of their pregnant bellies with the earth. We all drink tea and wrap ourselves in scarves and thick fisherman sweaters -- what a story the Irish yarn weaves in my mind, a stitch for each family's identification in the event of a sodden mishap, bloated bellies cradled in the soggy mass of cream-colored fibers, soaking in falling tears -- and rain jackets and wait for the drops to come. And when they finally do, the sky sends the wet screaming down as arrows, blunt and stinging nonetheless, and even though you spent the day in waiting, in knowing that the rain would come, it surprises you and sends you hopping for cover, yelping at the cold trickles down the back of your neck.

My cover came in the form of the used book shop, the solitary young clerk never flicking an eyelash at me as I entered, just sitting on a stool behind the till and reading some thick text, eating raisins from a plastic bag.

The shop felt warm after the sudden flood, rain needles still holding my skin tight in goose pimples. I wandered the narrow aisles, let my fingers brush over the spines crowded in together, organized just enough so that a shopper would know where to look for a mystery story or a Crocker cookbook, but still jumbled and thrown together in such a fashion that finding just the right book would be like an archae-ologist unearthing some crusty treasure from clinging earth, or like Arthur tugging forth the sword.

I found the Plath book tucked in between Louis L'amour and a thick exegesis of martial arts through the ages. I don't know how I even saw the book, thin and gray-spined and thoroughly unremarkable. But I did slid it out with my index finger and the back cover's surprising pink scheme drew me in and I opened to the first page and read. And the words waxed about executions and New York City and tendriled about my heart and I wanted to read more, so I did. I stood there, hair plastered to my forehead, coat dripping a little pool onto the creaking wooden floor, and read four chapters by the writer I'd known was a poet, but hadn't realized was also a novelist.

Finally I blinked out of my reverie and felt like I was a child caught trying to steal chocolate out of a candy shop, but the clerk still sat with his raisins and did not seem to care. So I walked to the till and passed the young man the book, which he did seem to mind, and we traded cash for goods and I walked back out into the rain with the book wrapped in a brown paper sack tucked between my arm and bosom, running through the drops for the car.

17

NAT

The girl flowed yoga in the cemetery. Nat watched through the viewfinder of her camera — *Lucy*, he reminded himself, *the camera's name is Lucy* — and pressed his index finger down into the shutter, releasing it with a *click-switch*, flashing across the lens like a guillotine.

It felt strange to him, to capture the scene with a camera. He had never been one for photography. He didn't like how, once you let the shutter fly, you couldn't see what had occurred, what happened to stamp itself in negative onto the film until you brought the used roll to the store and the pimply-faced photography specialist on call rubbed his fingers all over your work, and then could you really call it your own any more? Nat didn't know, and it seemed to difficult a dilemma to bother wrestling long with. He preferred his pencil and pen and papers covered over with scrawl by his own hand, for what it was worth. At least you could see what you were working with then.

But that morning Dee had knocked on his front door -- to his father's surprise, for no one ever knocked on their door, and the girl's easy smile as she stood so naturally on the stoop at the earliest hour she found respectable for knocking on doors seemed to set his father both on edge and at ease as he stepped past her on his way to the office -- and held Lucy up to Nat and asked him to photograph her.

"I'd do it myself," she said, "but I don't have a timer on there. Can you help?"

Of course he could help, and he did. And even though he knew nothing about photography and even though he thought that the Polaroids he sent spewing across the grass couldn't possibly be what she wanted, be any good at all, he stared through the viewfinder with a certain awe. He had never seen anyone do yoga before, but even if he had Nat was sure that no one could possibly look as graceful as this girl. Every square inch of her pale skin seemed to yearn for each pose, pushing and stretching, appealing to some higher plane, into the dark of his heart. Pose to pose she shimmered like water, a swan diving in a stoop for the earth, gliding up as a warrioress of the Amazon, reaching fingertips up and up until he thought the sky would trickle between her fingers, that she would cup fragrant blue in her palms and offer him a drink.

She breathed and folded and touched her forehead to the earth, resting as a child. Then she sat back up, cheeks flushed, already reaching for the scattered pictures.

"Well?" she said, a little breathless as she plucked them like daisies, "How was it?"

Nat didn't know how to answer the question. "What do you mean?"

"Did they turn out okay? Was *I* okay?"

"I don't know about the photos, but you looked . . . really cool." The words sounded lame even before he gave them voice, but he winced and tried to ignore them. "Where did you learn how to do all that?"

"My mother," said Dee, shuffling through the photographs. "These are great!" Her smile widened and Nat breathed with relief that he hadn't mucked up her endeavor, with lung-busting pride that he had made the redhead smile once again. "Really, you should try taking photos more often."

He smiled and shook his head. It was fine once in a while, but the page was for him and he was for the page. "Does your mom do yoga, too, then?"

"She's a yoga teacher. She really wants to open her own studio in town, but for now she's teaching at the Y."

Nat didn't know that there were people who taught yoga, much less had whole studios and storefronts dedicated to just such a thing.

"It's really cool," he said again, in spite of himself.

Dee shrugged. "I like it, but some people get really into it and go all silly. My mom's always going on about getting in touch with her inner divine and stuff like that."

"Weird," agreed Nat.

But as weird and new and somehow saffron-colored yoga seemed to him, Nat wanted to see more, learn more. He wanted the girl to close her eyes and let her heels root into the grass and earth, reach down and down until she was connected to the rabbits in their burrows, twitch-nosed, and worms and the dead in their coffins. To breathe oxygen to trade with carbon, breathe in droplets of wet and damp that hung as invisible baubles in the air, breath the clear blue of the sky. He thought that must be why her eyes were blue until he remembered that they were not, that they were really brown, brown as chocolate, as cake, as cream-dripped coffee and he thought it strange that he did not remember.

He wanted her to raise her arms like wings and lift her torso up and up and then fold forward as if her spine no longer fed from her crown to her tip-toes, eyes closed in deep calm, deep concentration, muscles both melting into the swan dive and molding it, hard and soft and effort and nature melding, boiling one into the other until what first seemed confusion he could find as calm, quiet, like the edges of a pool collecting the contents of a waterfall, bubbles churning into the lapping kiss of water on a beach of shining pebbles.

But she did not resume her yoga, a cross between gymnastics and ballet. The girl instead stared into a photograph, one of those he had snapped. She peered deeper and deeper into the plasticine image until her nose almost brushed the surface with an oil smudge, eyelids narrowing about chocolate irises, the brown he had forgotten and remembered.

"What is it?" he asked finally. Nat wondered if he'd done something wrong, ruining the film or her vision, killing the art planted in her heart with the ungainly traipsing of his shutter finger.

"Weird," she murmured without looking at him.

"Mm," Nat said, nodding. "Yoga." He hoped he sounded less dumb than he thought he did.

"Yeah," she said, voice coming as if from another continent. And then, "What? No, not the yoga." She blinked, eyes refocusing on the boy. "Although I guess yoga *is* kind of strange, isn't it?"

He shrugged. "Well, then what are you talking about? What's weird? I mean, to you." Nat frowned at the words jumbled like a puzzle that refused to fit together just right.

Dee bit her bottom lip, bent her head to study the picture once more before lifting her eyes to meet his gaze.

"Do you believe in ghosts?" she asked. Her voice quivered, and a light of excitement that gave Nat goosebumps seemed to play over her face.

"What do you mean?" The words dropped from his lips slowly, heavy with the pull of gravity, words as stones.

She blew upward, sending summer-damped coils of hair fluttering. "Just what I said, silly. Do you believe that there are ghosts among us?" She raised her voice melodramatically and seemed unable to repress the flash of a smile that dashed across her freckled face like August lightning. Then she swallowed and it was in chains again, but only just.

"No," he said in a flat voice. "Don't be ridiculous." And it was true, he didn't believe in ghosts — or it was true until that night, when it had felt like his mother was there in his bedroom, bending over him, pressing the pillow into his face, his eyes, his breathless mouth. *But that was a dream*, he told himself, *just a nightmare*.

That's what his father had said, too, but Nat could tell that the man didn't quite believe his own words. *And he would know, wouldn't he?* thought Nat. Adults always seemed to know things like that, and since his father worked with the dead it seemed to the boy that he should be a special expert on the matter.

"Ridiculous? Come on, you've never wondered about ghosts and the afterlife and all that? In a place like this?" She raised her arms, gesturing at the slabs of etched granite rising and falling and rising across the manicured green.

"The dead are just dead. Empty and heavy and sort of crusty," said Nat. "That's it. My dad dries them and dresses them up and puts them in their coffins, and then he puts them in the ground. He's done it his whole life, and so did my grandfather, and *his* father, too. It's what I'll do, one day, I guess. And I've never heard a thing about ghosts." *Except except*, piped a little voice from somewhere at the back of his brain, *don't you mean except?*

Dee considered the boy, seeming to deflate, but only a little, Polaroid still quivering between index finger and thumb. Then, after a long moment, just when Nat began to squirm under her furrowed gaze, she said, "I don't know. I don't know if I believe you."

"You think I'm lying." *Because you are*, came the tiny voice again, *if only a little*.

"No," she shook her head. And then, "Are you?"

"What do you think?" He tore at the grass, sending a confetti of green blades flying over his crossed legs.

Dee rolled her eyes. "Whatever. I just meant that there must be more to the end of life than death, there's got to be something *after*."

"Sure, heaven," said Nat, "maybe, and hell, too. But that's different from saying you believe in ghosts. That's like saying Santa Claus and leprechauns exist."

"So?"

"So it's stupid. And it makes no sense."

"Says you." Her raspberry colored lips coiled into a scowl.

"Yeah, I do. And like you said, don't you think I should know something about death?"

She shrugged. "Maybe."

Nat glared at the girl, her face now closed to him, his own fingers ripping at the grass of their own accord. The silence grew about the pair, starched and crackling with invisible shocks. Dee stared at the photo, but he could tell that she wasn't really looking at it because her eyes stuck fixedly at one point instead of roving as they had just a few minutes ago, brown and light and alive.

And he sat and picked at the grass and at his sneakers and thought about walking away and leaving her and her ridiculous fantasies there, except – *except except except* – for the question that begged to be loosed, to be asked against his best knowledge and better judgment. He almost left, almost, but just as he let his brain wander to what he could do with the dwindling day, where he could perch a while and write or read, he heard a voice, his voice, leap to a grudging Judas life.

"Why?" He could have slapped himself for the word, for the way he hung for her reply and tried to pretend without success at uncaring. "Why do want to know what I think about ghosts?"

She blinked, and her mouth softened a bit. "Because," she said after a moment, "I think there's a ghost in this picture."

18

MIA'S JOURNAL

Awake all night, sick. I told Don it is displaced morning sickness, but I know better. I know how much a hand I have in this. Foolish, stupid, selfish -- that's my way.

I went to the doctor earlier. It always surprises me how I expect the office and examination rooms to be cold and stark and smell of ammonia, for the stirrups to be cold against my heels, and then it never is, but instead the nurses usher me about with maternal warmth that I can believe and the only goose pimples on my skin are from my embarrassment at being touched in such a private place by another man than Don, a man who is and is not a strange. The doctor told me to gain weight otherwise I'd put the baby in danger.

So I did. I went home and ate and ate, in secret, in silence, before Don made his way in from the dead. Everything my fingers could touch, could throw to my lips in a kiss that devours and devours. And when I felt full I kept on eating until my stomach stretched from the food more than from the fetus, until it felt like the masticated mass was lodged at the bottom of my esophagus, awaiting admittance into the next stage of the digestive passage. Still, I didn't stop, not until I nearly vomited, but didn't. I don't know why I kept the food down. Perhaps I couldn't bear the thought of expelling what I had just furiously stuffed down inside myself. It was — is — mine, somehow.

Until later. When Don came home and found me on the couch, holding my aching belly and telling him it was nothing, it was normal, of course. He believed me and brewed some tea for me, for us, and I hated myself for the lie and hated him, a little, for his kindness. Then he went for a shower and while the water crashed through the pipes I went into the bedroom, into my dresser and extracted the bottle of pills I keep in a pair of green rolled socks and swallowed four. "Fast-acting," the label says, "All-natural."

There is nothing natural about this. Everything in my belly, my intestines, gurgles as the laxatives hurry what was once food along, a twenty-four hour crawl made in six, or less, and I feel that I can't move from my toilet squat as it all runs out of me in a brown mess, sticky and explosive. I can't imagine how Don sleeps through it all, but somehow he does. I feel dirty.

The insides of my eyelids scrape across my irises as sandpaper. I still can't sleep, even though the flood has trickled to the odd grumble, a flipping in my abdomen that has nothing to do with the life that is — that is?? — still growing, still living there. I am tired. How do I presume to soil the temple this way? Shouldn't God strike me down? I feel almost that I want him to, that I need the smiting. This child is not worthy of love.

I want to be normal, and don't at the same time. I want to be healthy and whole, but not fat, but I don't think I can walk that too-thin knife edge. Don says I'm lovely, it's my heart he married and the rest is extra, but how can that be when men like to look at a woman's flesh? And mine feels so grotesque at times that I can't help how the monstrousness of my bulging skin bleeds out and out until all can see and know the real me.

Lord, I didn't ask for this. Save me, please. The life in me hurts so as it consumes.

19

NAT

Nat stared at the girl, at the back of the photo she held in her hand. The words, the outrageous statement, hung in the air and seemed to grow louder and louder in the silence until they filled all of the space between Nat's ears and outside of them.

Finally, he smiled. He didn't mean to. But the boy felt his lips splitting open, splitting apart, teeth bared in a grimace that barely felt like a smile even to his own mouth. He hated to think of what it looked like, what he looked like, but even so the edges of his lips continued to draw towards his ears, and his throat belched forth a grating bark of a laugh.

"A — ghost?" he said, voice high and strained. "That's impossible."

"Maybe," Dee said in a soft voice. "Maybe it is. Impossible." She said the word slowly, rolling it around in her mouth as if tasting it as she let it fly. "Ridiculous, even. But that doesn't make it less true."

"You're wrong. You're wrong." The words kept on in Nat's brain, a cadence that he held tight to. And beyond that his own pleading half-realized hope, *Please, please let her be wrong*. He didn't see how he could live in this place with spirits wandering, touching him without his knowledge. He suppressed a shudder, but barely.

"Just look, will you, instead of us going on and on like this." She shook her head as the photo stretched toward him, pinched between her thumb and index finger.

The boy considered it as if it were some filthy and diseased thing. He didn't want it, didn't want the Polaroid on him or near him. He knew that once he looked, that would be it — the image, however, terrifying or benign, would be chiseled into his brain forever. *Or at least for a good long while*, he decided. Longer than he wanted it to hover at the edge of dreams, or at the center of sweaty nightmares. Nightmares about her, about his mother. *A dream, a dream,* he reminded himself, *she was just a dream*. And, *Oh, please, a dream.*

Dee opened her fingers and the photo fluttered earthward, lighting on the knee of his jeans like a butterfly. He felt sick, the faint taste of bile beginning to rise at the back of his throat. Swallowing once, then again, Nat commanded his hand to quit its trembling, and picked up the plastic square.

Up to meet his gaze the black on white back rose, and then a flip to the image, captured red coils curled about a backward bend, spine a rainbow spanning a haze of grass. It all seemed normal, delightfully and wonderfully normal, without ghosts or demons or some other haunting horror. He opened his lips, his true-smiling lips, now, to tell the girl, to dismiss the thought, once and — happy day! — forever, forever ever and ever, ridiculous, it *was* ridiculous, he had known, he knew now, and —

His eye caught a blur to one side of the photograph, a blur that he had not seen at first. Not the haze of overexposure, not something to be counted as the Polaroid's lens or fuzzy, antiquated nature. It was a wisp, rising from the earth, pale and thin as silver-gray smoke. He would have thought it smoke if he didn't already know that the pair had burned nothing, and if a pair of dark eyes didn't stare out from the crown of the tendril. Tall enough to be a person, or the soul of a person or whatever it is that ghosts or spirits or specters are, but Nat could have brushed that away if not for those eyes. He felt his queasiness return, redouble, and this time he had to swallow again and again and again and clench his fists into balls to keep the bile back.

He looked up at the girl, who stared back at him. "See?" she whispered, voice hoarse and he wondered for the first time if she was scared, too. "You see it, don't you? The figure there, to the side of me? And the face?"

Nat didn't want to give his affirmation, to make the image that much more real, but he couldn't lie, and didn't want to, anyway. So he nodded. "Yeah. Yeah, I see it."

"Wild, isn't it?"

The boy shrugged. He didn't know what Dee meant by that. He opened his mouth to say as much, but then found that he didn't have the breath, didn't have the heart for it.

"I wonder who it is." Nat had to strain his ears to hear the murmured words.

"What do you mean?" he croaked.

"Who the ghost was before it was a ghost. When she was alive."

Nat's head jerked up. "She?" He pushed back the memory of the nightmare that seemed too real to be a real nightmare, tried to shut his mind against it.

"I don't know." Dee shrugged, shaking her head. "It seems like a girl, or a woman, I guess, to me."

"How can you tell?"

"I don't know," she said again. "Maybe something about the eyes? And a feeling, just a feeling." Her eyes wandered to the headstones surrounding them. "Do you think she's buried here?"

The boy swallowed. *Yes,* he answered his friend silently, *yes, I do, if the ghost is who I think it might be. She is here, her body. We put it in the ground here, me and Dad and the pastor.* But he didn't say any of that. Instead, he shrugged and didn't meet her eyes and muttered something about how the ghost could belong to anyone.

"Maybe," mused Dee. "Although it might make more sense for her to belong to a body that's buried here. I mean, what else would make her come here?" She bit her lip, brows knitting into each other in thought. "Or maybe she's from before this place was a graveyard at all. Maybe she died here, or lived here, or both, or —"

"Maybe it's us," Nat said, surprising himself with the volunteered conjecture. "Maybe it's connected to us or something."

"Could be, although what would a dead person want with one of us?"

She's angry, thought the boy, forearms prickling into a thousand tiny bumps. *I've done something, somehow, to her or to Dad and now she's mad.* But he couldn't imagine what he did, what it was possible to do to make the dead angry enough to rise.

Then he remembered that he'd hurt his friend, in his mother's name no less, even if Dee hadn't known it, and his heart sank like a stone.

"But I guess we'd better not forget that idea." Dee was still talking, words flying faster now as she chased theories along her own synapses. "It could come in handy later or be important. Or be right, for that matter."

Nat managed a little half-smile, but she didn't pause or even flick an eyelash in acknowledgement.

"I mean, we don't know *anything*," she said. "I wonder if anyone around here has ever studied ghosts and hauntings and stuff. Do you think there would be books on ghosts in the library?"

He shrugged. "I don't know. I've never looked."

"Well, we should. Look, I mean. Although we might end up writing our own book. It doesn't seem like something grownups would be very curious about."

"No," he agreed in a soft voice, knowing that his dad wouldn't be curious — and wouldn't like his son looking into this, not even a little. He swallowed hard as Dee chattered on, oblivious as Nat sank into himself.

DON

Don dabbed the menthol cream beneath his nose and inhaled the aroma that seemed to chill the inner canals of his nose, stretching into his brain, down the back of his throat, tickling at the roots of his eyeballs. Another deep breath, lungs welcoming the almost-burning scent, and another and he prepared to dress the baby.

Days like this he wanted to quit, wanted to walk away and leave the family business even though he enjoyed it most of the time, even though it had been the duty of the men of his family since before stepping onto the New World soil. The infant rested on the steel table, limbs sticking out too stiff, too straight, tiny death reflected on the silver expanse. The man's stomach turned at the thought of touching the thing, and some part of his brain marveled that he should be so squeamish and fussy, he who had prepared countless human shells for the final repose, people who had died in far more grotesque a manner. Death done by violence, the plunging of steel blades through skin, through veins and capillaries and arteries, deflating lungs, splitting eyeballs and stirring nerves and synapses and sticky gray matter. Gunshot wounds, severed limbs, old fashioned beatings carried past the point of thought or reason. Accidents, cars opening to the night after smashing into trees, waters, other cars, occupants burned by airbags and igniting engine fluid. The quieter diseases, microscopic beasts devouring a body's organs and energy, cancer tinting the skin to jaundice, a spew of bile before shrunken, shrinking death, lips peeled from teeth, death kiss lurid, garish on his table.

And yet none of that bothered Don. *Or perhaps*, he thought as he stood two arm's lengths from the stiff infant corpse, staring at how its fingers grasped at the cool and sterile air, *perhaps it gets to the man Don, but not the mortician. Maybe there are two, two parts of me, separate minds and pulses that trade this body out*. He wasn't sure if he liked the idea.

He sighed and stepped forward, gripping the under edge of the steel workbench cradling its grim and heartbreaking charge. The children, the babies, they were the worst. Even when their still faces lay otherwise unmarked in death, bodies not defiled by gore or marks of medical infiltration, Don could hardly stomach the business. These were the only cases he still used the menthol for, these too-young corpses. Anything for distance, to claim the slightest purchase on blessed distraction, to keep memories from tumbling down from their carefully forgotten keeping places on the highest dusty shelves of the man's mind.

But none of it ever works, and a sigh broke over the mortician that made his wide back shudder. *Not the ointment or music or all the meditation I learned and practiced just for this. I always remember. The ghosts always rise.*

He could no longer see the dead child. Stretching latex gloves over his fingers, letting them snap about his wrists, the hot tears came in falling floods, stinging a very little in the quiet, stinging not quite enough.

21

NAT

Nat stared up at the ceiling. Gray blue shadows stretched across it, long and wild to his wide eyes. Every night, each creak and groan of foundation and timbers, normal enough and ignored in the sun's light, crashed and bellowed against his eardrums. With each new noise his heart froze, then leapt in its hopscotch journey.

Is it her? he asked the gloom as his nerves jangled, *Has she come?* And then, his own brain in reply, *There's no such thing as ghosts, don't be stupid, stupid.* But that belief, held so easily in his decade of life that he'd hardly even noticed it before, seemed emptier, more hollow every time he grasped at it, like a reassuring mug of hot cocoa grown tepid.

The night spread itself about the boy, the room, the cemetery, thicker and deeper as the he lay, refusing to reveal if the phantoms that gathered at vision's edge were in his head or in the room, and he felt unsure of which was the worse.

MIA'S JOURNAL

I am really sick this time. Legitimately, actually, of the non-self-inflicted variety. Enough to wake up here, in a standard-sized bed that is not my own, surrounded by tubes and plastic sacks of fluids and machines that beep and buzz to the chatter of this body. It makes me want to cheer, almost, if only I could lift my hands, my head, without this ache screaming from every muscle called to the task, without the burning fatigue that has claimed this set of bones and skin and sinew. And the pain, hot and queasy in my belly, I could do without that as well. But even so, in the light of all that tender truth, I am glad in the knowledge that I did not do this to myself. It is nature at work, or the environment or stress or something else entirely, or a fancy cocktail of multiple somethings. It wasn't me.

Don is talking to the doctor in the hallway. I can hear their voices, deep and masculine and soft, the haze of conversation filtering through the fissure where the door meets its resting place. I don't know what they're saying, can't make out the words. In fact, it comes to me again that I don't know why I am here, in this hospital, in the first place. I wonder what happened. I can dredge up last shreds of memory — scooping piles of wrinkled laundry from the hamper into the washing machine, pushing the fabric down into the hot water alive with foam and soap. But from there, I don't know what the next steps of my dance could have been to land me in this place.

It smells in here. I can already smell how the scent of urine, human feces and pasty medications and trays of mass-produced nutrition have worked their way into my hair. Eau d'hospital. Or something like that, I was never much good with foreign languages. But it could be worse, of course, of course it could always be worse, and I didn't do this to myself and that is the best, worth foul-smelling pillow hair and even this pain, stabbing in my belly, sharper with every breath. I wonder what they're talking about in the hall, why it's taking so long. I wish they would come in. It hurts, hurts more when I'm alone with the machines and monitors. God is here, I know, but the edges of vision grow darker and where is he where where is Don —

23

NAT

"Any more run-ins with ghosts last night?" asked Dee.

The two were sitting on the step just outside the kitchen door, the after-school sun still thin and damp and tasting more of autumn than it had yet that season as it spread across their shoes, the lawn, the span of headstones casting groping shadows. The house stood silent and empty at their backs, the boy's father already tucked into his office in the next building over.

Nat shrugged. "I didn't sleep, or at least I didn't sleep very much."

"Because of ghosts?" Her eyes widened.

He shook his head. "No. Just . . . me, I guess. Being stupid." He traced thin and chalky designs onto the stoop with a shard of stone.

"Why do you think you're stupid?"

He knocked the stone against the rise of poured concrete. "Because," he said, shoulders hunching into another shrug.

The girl waited. He could feel her brown eyes boring into his face, somehow easy and intense in the same moment. "Because I should know better." The words seemed to burst from him.

"That doesn't make any sense," Dee said, making his lips twist in annoyance. "We both saw the picture. Doesn't that sort of prove that ghosts are real?"

"I don't know." He rolled his eyes. "It's not exactly definitive evidence."

"I think it proves something. So if ghosts are real, you're not stupid." Dee crossed her arms as if she had proved some great and weighty thesis with an unshakeable conclusion.

The stone scratched white from Nat's hand. "I don't know. The photo wasn't all that clear, it's probably just a coincidence or something. But I shouldn't let myself get all weird about ghosts and dead people and all that."

"Why not? I would feel creeped out if I had to live here." She raised her shoulders in a little shiver, red curls falling down her back.

"Yeah, most people probably would. But I'm not like you, or them. I've always lived here, and it's never scared me or freaked me out, not even when —" He cut off, sucking in his breath as the bottom of his stomach seemed to drop suddenly open.

"Not even when what?"

Nat's mind filled with his nightmare, the feeling of cotton still heavy on his tongue, with the hazy figure in the photograph, the eyes, the *eyes*. His blood flowed hot and then cold and then burned in his veins again as he opened his mouth and let himself tell the truth. "When she died."

The girl swallowed, and then, almost as if she didn't want to loose the question but at the same time couldn't help but ask, learn, know, "Who?"

His voice came as a hoarse whisper grating up from his gut. "My mother."

Dee said nothing. A strand of copper found its way to her lips and she sucked on it until it shone dark and wet. The boy felt her eyes on him, but they were not as heavy as before and he did not mind. He even enjoyed their feathery non-touch, in a way. It felt something like when his father rubbed his back when he was sticky and sick with a stomach flu.

The sunlight grew colder, the light thinning as its source sank toward the earth, toward the house and the office with its connected laboratory-like workshop, the spread of head-stones almost cheerful. The shadows the markers cast grew longer in the wearing on of the afternoon in to evening."

"She died," Dee said after what seemed to Nat both a vast while and only a moment.

He swallowed. "Yes."

"When did she – when did it happen?"

"Four months ago next week." The boy did not have to think about, to calculate the months and days and hours, the minutes that he had lacked a mother. He knew it just as he knew his own age, when Columbus found what everyone thought at the time was India, the date of Christmas.

"Why? What happened to her?"

Nat shook his head. A sideways glace showed him Dee's knit brows, creased forehead. "I don't know. Not the whole story, anyway. My dad didn't want to tell me then, thought I wasn't ready for it, maybe, and now I think he just wants to forget it all. But —" he paused, swallowed again "— she killed herself. At least, I think she did. That's part of it, somehow."

"But you feel like there's more to it?" Dee asked in a small, even voice. "Like there's more to the story?"

He nodded, a single jerk of his head to the clouds and blue above. "Yeah. Like that. There's something else, maybe."

"What do you think it is?"

"I have no idea," he sighed, a great rush of breath. "And don't think I haven't tried to figure it out, either. But I just don't know."

Dee folded her knees close in to her chest, wrapping her arms around then and clasping her dimpled elbows. She rested her chin on her knees, mouth thin and long and Nat could almost see her brain working away at the question behind her eyes. "Well," she said finally, "maybe that's why she's here. If the ghost is her at all, I mean. Maybe she wants you to know, or maybe she's sad that she — that she left you and your dad and she wants to say sorry."

"Maybe," Nat said. He rubbed at his eyes with the heels of his hands, and the sandpapery relic of his sleepless night felt satisfying and deep. If the ghost was his mother, and if the nightmare of a week ago — *a week already?* he realized — was not a nightmare at all, the boy didn't think Dee's theory was good for much reassurance.

I wonder if I'm safe, he thought. And then, *I wonder if I should tell Dad*. But even in the idea of it, tucked safely inside his brain, the words he would stumble over in the telling to his father sounded thick and dull and altogether ridiculous. Maybe he would tell his dad, if he and Dee found out something more, or if something happened to Nat — he swallowed hard at the thought — but not now. It was too easy for the boy to imagine the hurt and concern he would see on his father's face, and he felt ashamed.

"Maybe we should just leave it," Nat said, queasy again. "Let's just forget it, okay?"

"But," said Dee, eyes as saucers, "this could be really important. Maybe she needs help, the ghost. Even if it isn't your mom."

"Whoever or whatever the ghost might be, if it's anything at all and not just some smear in your camera, it's dead and gone and probably buried somewhere. There's not much you can do for dead people."

"But what if there is?"

He jumped to his feet, anger flaring up in his chest. "I don't care," he said in a choked voice, hands balled into fists at his sides.

And then, remembering the last time he had been angry with Dee, remembering how his knuckles had met with her freckled cheek, he stumbled back a pace, afraid of himself. Breath ragged and shallow, feeling as if every bit of his skin was shelled in gray cement, he turned toward the house and went inside, letting the screen door swing shut with a rattle and bang.

The girl sat, still and pale on the stoop. The sun sweltered and inched closer to the zenith. No breeze ruffled the cropped grass. Inside, the boy lay face-down on his bed and let the pillow catch his tears. He did not see when the crimson-haired figure stood, dusted the backs of her legs and began to thread her way through the gray stone sentinels, heading for home. Sleep came to him at last, deep and dreamless as the grave.

2 4

DON

Soft leather swelled around him. Books lay open on the wide desk before the man's unseeing gaze, scattered and jockeying for position, over and under and overlapping. Personal schedules and cemetery calendars and financial notebooks and scratch paper worked over in figures, hand-etched calculations and winding curlicues. Procedure manuals, black- and brown-backed thicknesses stacked along the shelf facing the desk, a wall of leaves. A slim cup cradled a handful of identical pens, and a lamp with a bronze base rose from the desk's cluttered surface to penetrate its ivory dome shade. The light was off, the morning sun washing across the room.

Don let his eyes wander the spread, but they could not find a resting place. The office usually stood in quiet order, ready to envelope mourning clients in its oaken comfort, the vague scent of cinnamon emanating from the air freshener plugged into a wall behind the rise of a potted shrub. He did not know what kind of plant it was. It had been a gift from some grateful customer or other, and its thick and shining leaves spoke to him of an arid place of snow or sand. The thing didn't seem to mind his spare waterings of it, anyway. He rubbed a hand over his eyes, feeling the bristly prickle of his salt and pepper brows.

It had been a busy week. A difficult week. Later that day, in the afternoon, he would bury the infant. The lift already waited to rock the tiny coffin in its metal arms to the sound of the mother's sobs, ripping from a throat already raw from tears, from the tears of the next days and months and hours, as the machine lowered the coffin into the earth. The hurt would numb, he knew, he had seen, but never disappear, and in a year or ten that mother would see a baby dressed in the same lavender she buried her own in and the tears, the rising bile in her esophagus would be as hot and bitter as they are today. He knew, saw, had seen.

And there would be the father's mute nods at friends and family crowding in to rub his black-suited forearm while his fingers dangled helpless, without comfort for his wife, his tears already spilled at the hospital, the morgue, the other side of Don's typically immaculate desk as he signed the client copy of a receipt for the dead child's casket.

A girl, Don reminded himself of the dress he had shrouded its — *her* — pale form in the previous day, purest cotton the color of frost-kissed mountain flowers. His fingers dug into his eye sockets again. *Baby girl girl girl*, his brain chanted at him. He checked the delicate silver clock that faced him from the opposite wall's tome-stacked bookcase. Three hours until the black-vested procession burst forth from a stream of cars united by ignited headlights, so many salt-streaked ants. Three hours seemed a precipice of time that wrenched his gut with that feeling of falling, too long to pass in this life, but too short to gather himself and become the solid, the dry-irised pillar holding up a bit of sky while the mourners gathered at the graveside and shattered at their heartbreak.

A notebook, hard bound and wrapped in cornflower colored fabric, lay open across the stacks of figures and contracts and receipts, his fingers light against the exposed ocean of ball point writing. Line after line of regular rising, falling documentation of a life, on and on backwards into a memory not his own.

Don didn't know why he still read them, his dead wife's journals. And why he read this one particular, this account of her darkest time that cut him to the soul. But it was a connection, a disturbing one, to be sure, but a lifeline to feeling like the woman he loved wasn't too far away. He wasn't ready to let her memory grow distant, not yet.

He ran his tongue over dry and splitting lips and read, following the neat script beyond himself into shattered heart of the past.

25

NAT

Nat walked home from school in the afternoon warm light. As he paced up to the little white house, he could see a funeral party huddled together out on the grounds, attended by his father's tall form. Even from this distance Nat saw how carefully the man folded his fingers together in front of him.

But he barely heard the murmur of the final passage rites that filtered into his ears. Seeing that his father was occupied, and would be so for a while longer, he jogged across the graveyard straight as a loosed arrow in the opposite direction. His arms pumped at his sides, and he knew what he wanted to do. But first he needed to find Dee.

He still didn't know where she lived. Nat didn't quite know how that was possible. She always seemed to be hanging around the cemetery, the two of them sprawling a picnic lunch across some resident's bed, or her red-haired form flitting among the stones with the Polaroid, Lucy. His father had granted her polite request to do this with his blessing, a small and — Nat thought at the time — sad smile passing across his face as he told the girl to make sure not to interfere with visitors and, of course, funerals. She obeyed with care, although she hadn't taken pictures lately. *Not since the ghost*, Nat thought. *Since it came to us, and Lucy, too.*

The boy didn't much like the thought of living at the whim of the ghost — or ghosts, he supposed, because who was to say that there couldn't be more where one had already walked? *If it was a ghost at all,* the boy he reasoned with himself as he jogged down one street and across another. And that was part of the plan his brain formed in the still moments between waking and slumber, so that by the time his eyes had opened fully that morning, he knew what he wanted to do. What he needed to do.

He wouldn't, even couldn't, maybe, do it alone. *Besides, Dee would kill me if I tried. One more ghost to haunt this place.* And then, cringing at the thought, at the fact that it crossed his mind so naturally, so easily, *But then maybe I'd be able to see* her, *talk to her.* His mother, the ghost, the dead one.

When she died, he'd cried at first, tears that seemed to burn twin trails into his cheeks. He still felt them, sometimes. And then, after he'd shed more tears than he thought his body had the water to spare for, he hated her. Just a little at first, a pinprick of anger, and later turning, stoking itself into a bonfire that reached from the pit of the pit of his stomach up past his lungs, filling them with black and acrid smoke, up through pumping blood and the closing of his heart's chambers to the dry churning of his brain as he watched his father strong shoulders crumple a little more every day. And Nat had wondered, then, if seeing Nat each morning as he spooned Cheerios between his lips, stumbling from the afternoon school bus daily, tucking his son every empty evening without her, if all that made the mourning and moving on harder for his father, if the man came to hate Nat like the boy hated his mother for leaving them, leaving him to grow up alone.

How could she? he asked himself or the clouds or the last ranks of dead for the millionth time as he navigated toward what he hoped was Dee's street. *How could she let herself die? Did she even try to get better?* And then answered some part of his brain that he had trained into muffled silence most of the time but still every now and again whispered as horribly, mutinously as it did now, *You weren't enough. You weren't enough to make her want to try, to take care of herself, to keep herself alive.*

And just as he always did, Nat narrowed his eyes and the corridor of his brain so that he could better control what thoughts squeezed through into his awareness and pushed back at the voice and his anger and the memory of his mother's pale and pinched face framed by the even whiter spread of the hospital pillow case, back down to wherever it lurked, waiting for its next chance to break for freedom.

Dee, he told himself, and then aloud, a mutter, "Where would she be . . . ?" The last time he had tried to find her, she had met him on the way. But now the black asphalt was empty of humanity, his own aside, in the late afternoon. *Not so lucky, not this time.*

He scanned the front yards he passed, suburban in their sameness, in their careful differences. Manicured squares of lawn, landscaped, shaped with hedges, crab apple trees, geraniums and gardenias, all new-planted, with the seasoned oak and maple trees standing sentinel at deliberate, falsely random intervals. These towering remnants made the boy think of long-bulldozed forests that once peopled this part of the land, before white skin, before ships sprouting masts and canvas and webs of rigging.

He searched for a sign, for clues that would point him to his friend. A sea green house with a too-cheerful garden gnome poised in leering welcome by the front step — she would tolerate the gnome, he decided. Nor would she allow a family of ceramic deer, and the driveway filled with sporting equipment — a pair of jet skis yoked to a trailer which in turn was connected to a massive pick-up truck that gleamed Hollywood red above oversized tires and spotless silver hubcaps that reflected the afternoon sun's glare straight into Nat's eyes – that didn't seem to speak of a home for Dee, either.

The long ranch style home that squatted at the end of the block, its blue paint too bold and stark to sit comfortably on the walls of a building, didn't feel like a place she would live. Its lawn was messy, or messier than that of its companions, weeds and errant tufts of grass growing every which way. And yet there she lay, belly up in the going-wild grass, camera pointed up at the sky. Nat hesitated at the curb, rocking from his sneakered heels to his toes and back again. He had pictured her home as immaculate, supremely tended. But perhaps that was because the cemetery was just that way. *She just moved here,* he told himself. *Maybe her family hasn't had a chance to do much yet.* And then another thought occurred, *Or maybe they just don't care.* He wondered if he cared.

He remembered his idea, the reason for his trek. Stepping onto the unkempt lawn, he waved a hand in greeting even though he knew the girl wasn't looking at him, wouldn't see it,

"Hey," he said.

Dee yelped and jumped a little, and then sat up, bits of yellowed grass stick out from her curls. "Oh," she said, blinking. And then, "Nat!" A smile blossomed over her berry lips. "What are you doing here?"

"Looking for you," he said.

"How did you even find the place?"

"Luck." He dropped to his knees at her side. "Listen. I've got an idea." The boy kept his voice low, even though there was no one around to overhear the conversation.

She raised her eyebrows, curiosity stealing into her eyes. "What kind of idea?"

"About the ghost, or whatever it is." He drew a deep breath. "I don't want to wait around to see what it is or if the thing will come back, and if it will be scary. And I hate feeling scared and worrying and thinking about it all the time, wanting to know what *it* wants and what's going to happen and what it thinks about us." *And what it's going to do* to *us,* he added in his head.

"So what do you want to do? It's not like we can make a date with it. At least," the girl said with a frown, "I don't think we can."

"Probably not. But I was thinking — what if we hunted it, instead of waiting for it to just pop up again? What if *we* go looking for *it*?"

"You mean like on those paranormal investigation shows?"

Nat nodded.

Her frown deepened. "I don't know. Do you think that would work?"

He shrugged. "Maybe. I've never done this sort of thing before. I don't know how it's supposed to work. All I know is that I'm tired of just sitting around and waiting."

"How would we hunt it? Or hunt any ghosts at all? Where should we go?"

"Well, our cemetery's probably a good enough place to start. And we can use your camera and take pictures of graves and stuff, since that's how we found the last one."

"But I've taken loads of photos there already, Nat. And it's only been the one that a ghost showed up in."

"Yeah," he said, nodding, "but we haven't taken any at night."

The girl stared at him. "At night?"

"Sure." Nat's voice sounded much braver than he felt at the thought of sneaking around in a graveyard after ghosts, especially after dark. "Isn't that when spooky stuff is supposed to happen? It always works that way in scary movies and books, and on those shows."

"I guess." She shook her head. "What will your dad say?"

The boy pursed his lips. He hadn't thought of that. "I don't know," he said after a moment. "He probably wouldn't like it much. We'd probably have to be sneaky about it. Besides," he nodded at the blue house, "what would your parents say?"

"Oh," she shrugged, "of course I wouldn't tell them. I don't think they would understand. But it's not their cemetery we're going to either."

He crossed his arms. "Well, what do *you* say, then? If we're careful and don't mess anything up and my dad never finds out — what do you say to that? Are you in?"

Dee considered him for a long moment, forehead crinkling a little. Then she stuck out her chin and nodded, once, twice. "Yes. Yes, I'm in." A grin flashed across her face. "I mean, how could I pass something like this up?" And then the grin was gone and a pale smile hung in its place and he could see that the girl looked as nervous as he felt, which was saying something because his insides were jiggling and squirming like a mass of worms. But the thought of passing any more nights damp in sweat at the thought of what phantom should-be-dead *thing* might come into his bedroom, come for him — that felt worse.

"When do you want to do it?" she asked.

"Soon." Nat thought for a moment. His father had another funeral scheduled for the following morning, so that put this night out. He didn't much like the thought of traipsing through the cemetery with open graves lying about. The boy shuddered at the thought of spending the small hours of the morning dark at the bottom of a dank and new-dug grave. But the next day, the day after tomorrow, he knew that no funerals were happening then. "Tomorrow night," he said, nodding his head in decision. "We'll do it tomorrow night."

"At midnight?" She shrugged at Nat's raised eyebrows. "Like you said, creepy things always happen at midnight in the movies."

The boy inclined his head. "At midnight," he echoed, and even though his knees felt like limp spaghetti strings at the thought of their impending adventure, he also felt stronger, glad that that they could try something, that he could *do* something. "Midnight tomorrow," he whispered and flopped back onto the too-long grass, the sunlight turning the insides of his closed eyelids crimson as embers.

MIA'S JOURNAL

I felt well enough to stand this morning. The blonde nurse — who seems too young to be able to drive to the hospital by herself let alone work here — she got angry at me when I told her that I used the bathroom by myself.

"You need rest," she said, shaking her head as she fiddled with the bedside monitors, "and to get rest you need to stay in bed. You're not just taking care of yourself, remember."

As if I need the reminder. Of course it's not just me who's stuck in this bed, in this chilly, green-papered room. And no one has told me when I can go home to my own bed, to the cemetery, to my husband. Or, for that matter, what's gone wrong in me in the first place. If they don't know that — if I don't know it — how can we fix the problem? But the nurses won't say, the doctor never lets me slip a word much less a question in around what he surely thinks is a pleasant drone. And Don — well, he just sits at my bedside, pale faced and more sickly looking than I feel, and every time I ask his cheeks turn a little green, matching the walls like a chameleon, and his eyes slide away as he mumbles something or other about "inconclusive data," whatever that means.

But I can't just sit here, waiting for answers, for the right questions, even, and do nothing. I hate the nothing more than being poked with needles, more than the never-lessening pain in my stomach, more than being tied into the mass of snaking tubes at the side of the bed, more than I hate the bed itself, which you would think would be comfortable and orthopedic when really it is an unyielding foam mattress spread with sheets and covers that feel like they are made from cardboard. So I got out of this awful bed, stood — or swayed, really — on my own feet.

I had to pee. The bed pan is a humiliating invention. Shining steel cold against my bedridden behind, it represents how very useless I am, how I am a burden to everyone around me, even to myself, to the baby. It reminds me, fresh, hot urine sloshing, swirling about its wide basin, how I cannot even do for myself one of the most basic acts there is that is still an action, like eating or sleeping. I don't know how the nurse can take the soiled thing without even a bat of disgust caught in her eyelashes, without wrinkling her nose and throwing the whole thing back at me, spilling my waste over the polyestered bed, without tasting sick in the back of her throat. Or maybe she does but she hides it better than I know, better than I can myself.

Just sitting on the side of the bed, sock-clad toes barely brushing the floor, was hard. Wave upon wave of dizziness, black and blinding, crashed through me, around me, caught me in their wake so that all I wanted was not knowing. I almost lay back against the pillows, somehow so inviting despite their roughness, their unyielding bulk. But then, through the clearing of temporary blindness, I saw the disinfected bed pan waiting on the little taupe nightstand and I couldn't, just could not bear to use it again. So I stayed where I was, gulping in the air, ignoring the stabbing in my abdomen, the pressure and swelling there that seemed somehow unrelated to the life growing within.

*And after a little while — or perhaps a long while, I still am not sure
— of perching there, the bottoms of my feet seemed to drift down until
they were flat against the floor. I found myself, shaky, heart shuddering inside its cage, standing. Sliding one foot forward and then the
other, arms hovering around me seeking balance, ready to catch my
almost-certain stumble, I made my way into the tiny bathroom. With a
sigh I fell to the toilet seat and — who knew peeing could become such
a joy! I felt like I'd scaled Everest — let the waste fall into the waiting
pool. I didn't bother to close the door, for then I would have to open it
again and I still needed to get back to the bed. Which I did, flushing
the toilet, running water for a moment over my hands, which trembled
so much that I splashed wetness over the front of my standard issue
gown.*

*Turning, I saw on the floor next to the open door a little white scale.
Just an extra step out of my trajectory — what could such a tiny
detour do at that point? — so, leaning against the wall I stepped up
onto it. Strange how so small a step felt like a heaving scramble to my
spaghetti muscles. But I did it, and the numbers twirled like a compass
dial and informed me that I gained five pounds since I last weighed
myself. And that was — when, two days before I woke up in this
place? So at least a week, maybe more. Five pounds! It doesn't seem
possible.*

*But as I lay here in bed, this journal resting against my five-pounds-
larger belly, I feel — okay. I feel energy to stay awake and write, to use
the bathroom on my own again when I need to no matter what that
[probably] preteen nurse has to say about it, to go home and have a
baby and be a wife. Something in me is saying that those five pounds
can make me better, will make me better able to make it through this
maddening puzzle that is life. And that is somehow thrilling.*

*Why should that be? I find myself filling up with excitement at the
thought, at the idea that this just might be okay, that some good will*

have come out of this hospital stay that seems to linger on and on into an unknown duration. Strange, I think, but also good. Very good, in fact.

27

NAT

That night, the last and only night before the hunt, Nat could not sleep. He stared up into the gloom that pervaded the bedroom. Even while the shadows held unseen menaces that never used to be there, or that he'd simply never noticed, the darkness felt soft against his skin. He let himself sink into it, press in to its velvet warmth. *Tomorrow*, he thought, *twenty-four hours and I'll be getting ready to leave here, to go out* there.

Although he couldn't see them in the blackness, he could feel the spread of headstones and the dead they marked. Nat thought of all the scary movies he'd ever seen, ghost stories that he'd read or heard and wondered if they were true. Did the dead rise at night to stroll about the cemetery, unknown to its curators? He tried to imagine what the zombie dead would do, night after night and on into eternity. Chat with their neighbors, catch up on the latest worm gossip, or perhaps play a game of hide-and-seek among the grave stones? And if they did rise, what would they do to those who disturbed their gathering, to those whose hearts hadn't yet stopped, whose veins still coursed with hot blood instead of dank, pooling liquid? Would they be jealous of the living, would they try to steal back into life by snatching at his and Dee's breath, taking it for their own? Or would they even notice the interlopers?

That would be the worst thing, maybe, to meet with the apathetic dead. *Then we couldn't figure things out,* he thought, pulling the covers up to his ear as he rolled onto his side, *not if we can't find anyone or anything. If there aren't any ghosts at all.*

The boy didn't know what to hope for. Hunting ghosts, and then finding one or some or an army — he shuddered and pulled the covers up still higher. But if there was nothing, if all he and Dee discovered was the silent stillness of the graveyard beneath the stars and moon, quiet as it had always been, then they could draw no conclusions, and all his trembling and tenuous hoping would have been for nothing.

And would that mean I've been making the whole thing up all along? That I've just been imagining it? That there really are *no such things as ghosts and I'm just crazy?* He couldn't tell if he felt disappointed at the thought, and that made the contents of his stomach churn all the more. *But we've got to try. I've got to try to see her, to ask her* why.

He wanted an answer, wanted her to tell him, and if he had to wake all the dead in the cemetery to get it, well then, that's what he would do.

Tomorrow. Tomorrow night.

MIA'S JOURNAL

I woke to blood. The monitors barked like rabid dogs and the sheets were sticky around my legs. The nurse came in then, shouted for help. I don't know how she could, the metallic crimson stench choked me.

I can't write this. There are no words.

DON

Don thought the boy looked paler than usual on the other side of a steaming bowl of oatmeal.

"You okay, son?" he asked around his own mouthful of oatmeal, warm and comforting on its journey to his stomach, mixing with orange juice and coffee and sliced apple. *She always hated how oatmeal felt like it would stick to her insides* — the observation floated through his consciousness unbidden, and he let it flow by. *But I like it,* he called to the thought as it passed, almost lightheartedly teasing. Almost.

Nat blinked, then shrugged mid-chew. "Yeah. I'm okay."

The words did not convince his father that the dark circles beneath the boy's eyes were normal, that every spoonful of oatmeal hoisted to his thin lips did not feel like lead. "How are you sleeping?"

This time the boy looked almost guilty as he looked at his dad, then quickly dropped his eyes to his bowl. "Fine, I guess."

Don sighed and put his spoon down. He wondered if he should reach across the table, across the array of jam and juice and glasses and butter and brown sugar and the host of other morning condiments that spread out there like a chess match, and take his son's shoulder and squeeze life into the boy, squeeze some better version of the truth from him. But the man's own spoon felt too heavy in his hand, too, and he felt overly full of unknowing. And so he sat and ate, bite after agonizing bite, and did nothing else, stomach filling with oats and a sick and burning shame.

And then, "Maybe we should get you to bed a little earlier?" Nat shrugged again in reply. "We never did get back into the habit of going to bed at an earlier hour for school from this summer. It would be a good idea to start getting back into the habit of early rising."

"It doesn't feel like fall yet," Nat offered with a little sigh.

"It's coming, slowly. Soon it'll be so cold we hate it." Don wondered if the smile he pasted across his face looked as dull and limp as it felt.

Nat's spoon clattered to the side of his bowl. "Can I be excused?"

The man looked at the half-eaten oatmeal, the untouched apples and toast. "You haven't eaten very much."

"I guess I'm not that hungry."

"You know what I think about leaving food, Nat. It's such a waste." *But*, the man considered, *he really doesn't look like himself today.* "You may be excused — this once. Let's not make this a habit, okay?"

The boy nodded, and with two clicks of the door handle he was gone from the kitchen, slipping away into the thin morning air and off to school. Don sighed, put his own spoon. After a moment, he pushed back his chair and began to clear the table, spooning thick globs of oatmeal into the trash.

30

MIA'S JOURNAL

It's gone.

The baby. Fetus. The right word?

They tell me it was

would have been

a girl.

NAT

He found Dee with his mother. He knew they should be heading toward the school, but on his way down the drive he'd glimpsed Dee there with a little shock, at just that spot, his mother's spot, and he had to go to her. To them.

She sat before the rose-colored stone on the farthest end of the cemetery from the road, the house, the other residents. There stood just a small copse of saplings and a half-moon of rose bushes that Nat's father hoped would one day grow together into a hedge. *Her favorite flower, the yellow rose*, the boy recalled. Other family members rested nearby, but this spot was special. It belonged to her, just her. A single stone topped with an angel frozen in a pose of presumably helping his charge ascend from the world to some higher plane or place. It never did make Nat feel comforted.

She's supposed to be in heaven, he thought as he approached the figure clad in a cottony dress that billowed and spun about her solid frame, *Isn't that where dead mothers go?* It was what he'd always thought, what he told himself in the night when the house was too quiet and the loneliness threatened to devour him. But he didn't know how to believe that she rested in peace when he planned to hunt her ghost that same night.

"You found her," he said in greeting.

Dee looked up, pinching guilt resting for a moment at her chin. "Just introducing myself." She pointed at the marker's inscription, Polaroid camera balanced in the opposite hand. "Did you write this?"

He shook his head, the verses etched more firmly in his brain than the granite, it felt like.

Love and trust Him

sparrow heart

to feed your soul forever

and rest on.

"No, it wasn't me." The boy shrugged.

"So who wrote it?"

A sudden swelling in his throat. He swallowed, choking it down and back and down. "She did. She wrote it." His voice came off of his tongue thin and wavering.

"Oh." The girl reached out a hand, brushed it across the letters, the sterile numbers that spoke nothing about the dead woman's life. "It's lovely. The poem."

Nat shrugged. He couldn't separate the poem from the death marker, from his mother's leaving. "It's okay."

"Words must run in your family."

He raised his eyebrows at his friend, sinking into a crouch with his back to the headstone. "Does creativity even work like that?"

"I don't know." She grinned, and snapped her camera's shutter at Nat, the photo diving for the earth, exposing. "Does it matter? But it's cool, that your mom was a poet, and you are, too."

"I'm not a poet."

"But you write poetry."

"Well, yeah, but it's not all that great, and I don't write very often —"

"But you *write poetry*." She glared, daring him to challenge her. "Right?"

Nat glared right back at the girl, but he sensed that he didn't have much of an argument, especially against the stubborn wrinkle at the bridge of her freckled nose. He could feel his blue notebook curled in the back pocket of his jeans. "Yeah, but like I said, only sometimes —"

"Sometimes is more than never, and you are good with words."

"You don't know enough about poetry to say that," he said, shaking his head. "You're not an expert."

"Oh, and you are?"

"Maybe. Maybe I am."

"But you just said you're not a poet." Dee stuck out her tongue at him. He rolled his eyes and shrugged. "Ha!" she crowed. "I win. But I'm right, you know, for real. Words like you."

"Whatever." He grabbed the photo up from where the blades of grass held it aloft like a body borne to its final pyre.

It should have been unattractive. Inside the white-framed frozen world, his mouth hung open and his eyes seemed strangely unfocused. The sky behind him spread silver-bright despite the deepening blue that hung above them, bleeding across the cheeks of his photographed image, his lips, the tousle of uncombed hair. It should have been ugly, he should have scowled at it in vague embarrassment at how awful he looked, at what an unskilled photographer Dee must be to even consider such an unpracticed process. But somehow, somehow everything about the photograph spoke of the velvet rolling of heart thoughts, and the photographed Nat looked noble rather than dumb.

Then it all felt like too much, and he threw the plastic square away, diamond tumbling in brief flight.

Maybe Dee's not wrong after all, he thought to himself. *Maybe cameras, pictures, or whatever — maybe they like her. So maybe words could like me, too. Just like they liked my mother.*

Then he bit down on his bottom lip hard, too hard, tasting salt and pain and the iron in the blood now flowing into his mouth. The sight of the headstone suddenly made his belly flood hot and then freezing, cold and wet as February sleet, and he stalked away, refusing to even look back at the graven words that seemed to beg for his attention.

I will find you, he thought, relishing the tang of blood in the back of his throat. *I will, tonight or some other night, you won't be able to hide and I'll get my answers.*

"Nat?" Dee stared up at him, the discarded photograph dangling from her fingers. "Are you okay?"

"I'm fine." This time the words sounded gravelly, barely squeezing out from between his teeth as they ground up and down, molar against clenching molar. "Just fine."

"Um. You sure?" Her eyes flooded with — he hated to even think the word, to recognize it on another face, on *her* face when she was supposed to be his friend not just another offering of shallow, pallid pity for the poor kid that lost his mother, his sick in the head excuse for a mother.

He kicked at the grass and swore, and those brown eyes traded hurt for the worry. "Yeah!" he shouted, anger burning hotter at himself even while he could not seem to pull himself back from the brink of whatever cliff dropped away in his seething brain. "I'm fine! Or do you think I'm lying? That I'm some stupid liar?"

"No, that's not what I —"

"Well, thanks! Thanks a whole lot. You're my friend, or you're supposed to be, and then you call me a liar straight to my face like that." He stomped away, and then back, knowing how unfair he was being and yet unable to stop himself. He wanted to be alone, but couldn't bring himself to leave.

"I didn't! I didn't call you a liar, but come on, Nat, you're kind of getting scary." The words spilled from between her lips in a steady stream, freckles dark against her paling cheeks.

The word brought him up short. He stared. "Scary? I'm scary?" The bottom of his stomach felt like it opened up, letting all the poison that had been digested out of his system swirl back in, black and bilious and cold, cold against the temper. The two met with a crack, a titanic summer storm meeting in his gut. He wondered if he would be sick.

Dee shrugged. Then, sucking both her lips into her mouth, she nodded, fast. "Yeah. Sometimes, you are. When you're like this."

The cold and hot churned and churned in his belly, and the sudden thrill of pleasure at this new power the boy found he could yield made his whole frame vibrate with dark glory, with sickness at himself. *I'm worse than her,* he thought, and kicked at his mother's headstone. Dee flinched, and he realized what she must think, that it must look like he had aimed his sneakered blow at her and missed, and somehow that sent him reeling away.

"No," he said, throat raw and rasping all of a sudden. "That's not — no — I'm — I can't — I'm sorry —"

The words, or the right ones, refused to string together and he couldn't stand the burning of her swimming brown eyes on his skin any longer and turned and ran, feet pounding across the field. He didn't stop when his notebook fell from his pocket, when she cried for him to wait, when he tripped and stumbled blindly past the granite in teary blindness, the markers catching at his legs, bursting purple and blue green fireworks up and down his shins.

3 2

DON

The gray-haired man wondered if he held a demon in his
arms or a boy. Leaving the office to replenish his stock of
teabags, forgotten after the abandoned breakfast, Don had
seen his son tearing across the cemetery, colliding with what
seemed like every headstone. As he drew nearer the buildings
between which Don stood, the man could hear the cracking
of his shins and knees against the markers and he didn't
know what he should fear breaking more, the stones or
his son.

For a moment he thought that Nat was being chased by a
swarm of hornets, or that he had gotten something in his
eyes that burned and made him run for water. And, some
detached part of his brain wondered, why was't the kid at
school.

But then Don saw the grimace of anger and pain that filled the
boy's mouth, and he saw how purple his face and neck were. And
he remembered how Nat had been nearly fourth months ago
now, how, after her death, the boy had come home from school
day after day with fresh bruises circling his eyes, newly split lips,

relics of the fights he picked with older boys, larger boys, boys who could really lay on a beating. The school counselor recommended regular therapy, so that's what they had done, some sessions with Nat seeing the therapist alone, and some with Don present. At first the man was convinced that he'd lost both wife and child when he buried the woman he loved, that there was no calling Nat back from the constant pyre of rage he was seemingly all too happy to sacrifice himself on every moment.

But, days and weeks rolling themselves out in months, the boy became a boy again. Different from before, but Don expected that, accepted it. He would take any improvement over the animal Nat had become. The healing Nat, the new Nat, didn't have many friends left, but it was summer anyway. The boy wandered the headstones, which he had always ignored before, and scribbled in his notebooks. *This is better*, Don had always told himself, ignoring how pleading and plaintive the reassurance sounded even inside his head. *Better to be disconnected than in prison, in pain, or dead.*

But maybe Nat hadn't been healing after all, but had been hiding from the grief all summer, Don thought distantly as he ran out and intercepted his son, tackling him in a sort of embrace to keep him from running, keep him from hurting himself.

The boy-turned-animal clawed at Don's arms, his face, popping buttons off the man's shirt, every limb wheeling and spinning and alive. Don hung on, all of his weight and energy behind keeping his purchase on his son. He felt his breath come heavier, and he didn't know if it was from effort or fear or tears.

"Nat," he barked over the boy's pleas to let him go, to leave him alone. "Nat! Tell me, what is it? What's wrong? Nat?"

"Nothing! It's nothing. Just let me be!"

"This is not nothing! And I'm not letting you go. Not until you tell me. Let me help." He tried to keep his voice steady, to not yell, but it was nearly impossible as he jerked his head to keep a flailing fist from connecting with his chin.

Nat sank his teeth into his father's forearm. Taken by surprise, the man yelped and his grip loosened. Twisting, the boy spun away and ran. Holding his arm where Nat had bitten him with his opposite hand, Don watched the boy change his original trajectory, heading for the street instead of the house. He swore quietly.

Lifting his palm, another curse slipped from between his lips. Mirror half-moons on his arm oozed ruby beads, then trickles. He wondered if anger was transmittable by blood. *Like rabies*, he thought. He had prepared a rabies victim for burial once. That had not been pleasant.

The man still stood there, in a sort of shock, when Dee ran up, panting.

"Did you see him?" she panted, neck flushed from exertion but her cheeks pale beneath her scattered freckles.

He nodded. "He ran away." The man gazed in the direction his son had taken, wondered what the boy had taken into his fevered brain to do.

"What should we do?" She stared up at him, waiting, trembling visibly.

"Are you okay?" he asked, looking her up and down. *No injuries*, he sighed in relief. *At least, none that I can see.*

The girl's thoughts seemed to reflect his own. She nodded, but only after a long moment. "I'm fine." Her voice sounded flat. "What's wrong with him?"

Everything. Nothing. "It's grief." And then, "I need to make a phone call."

She followed him into the house without asking. He did not tell her to leave. Don was, he realized as he picked up the telephone, glad of the company.

"Who are you calling?"

"The police." It had been a while since he had last made this kind of phone call. The kind where he wasn't sure if he'd see his son alive again, or without handcuffs, without the stain of some other person's blood under his fingernails from yet another fight sought to ease his pain by inflicting it upon someone else. *But they'll remember,* he knew. *The police won't have forgotten so easily.*

"Is he in trouble?"

Don paused before dialing the final digit. "Yes." The phone began to ring. "He is."

"911, what is your emergency?" asked the voice on the other end of the telephone.

As Don began to explain, the screen door slammed shut from behind him as the girl disappeared in a swirl of color and the scent of strawberries, and the words he uttered in a voice thick with heaviness that even he could hear filled the empty kitchen.

33

NAT

There was only the running.

Sneakers slapping against grass against pavement *thwud thwud thwud thwack thwack* right left right left repeat again again run legs swish swishing one past the other arms tight muscled pumping elbows against ribs ribs inhale exhale repeat again heart beat heart blood beat beating on and on.

The boy couldn't stop. He didn't want to stop, but even if he had, he didn't know if he'd be able to. It didn't matter, not now, so he kept on and relished how pressure built in his belly, rising into his chest, how he felt as if his torso might burst in a fleshy firework of muscle and crimson and skin. He ran a flash of tongue along his lips, saliva congealing and drying there. Then he tripped and stumbled a little and his teeth clamped down on his tongue, ripping into it, and he liked how that felt, too, quick and sharp and salty.

He didn't know where he was going. That didn't matter, either. Certainly not to school as he was supposed to. *No destination. Just go, keep on going, go go go* chanted his brain in time with his foot slaps. Pavement unrolled before him, hot waves rising to press against his cheeks and pool between his knuckles. But his raging blood ran cold to the boy, goosebumps racing even faster up and down his arms, trickling along his spine, faster even than the rising of his knobbly knees, one after the other, on and on.

Houses and lawns and his brain latched for a moment onto a fat-bellied garden gnome, a fake deer family. Something about the deer irked him, twisted and pinched at his stomach and he shot across the front lawn of their home and crashed into them with a leap, tumbling to earth with their ceramic antlers and hooves and visionless eyes. And even as they still seesawed in the grass he untangled himself and was at them with his feet and ankles, kicking and punting and stamping until shards and shattered limbs stuck in the green blades. He felt the latch on the house's front door *slide click* and the opening yawn but he was already vaulting from foot to foot away and away down the street, refusing comprehension of the shouts hurled at his back.

The homes slid by on either side of his vision in a parade of muted, sedate colors. And then, a shock to the eyes, to the sensibilities of any sane person, Nat would have thought if he had allowed thoughts to squeeze into being, brightest blue. Gaudy and overdone, it assaulted some tiny chink in the boy's singleminded barrel and the the blue melted across his brain, sticky as new-spawned tree sap in the fall.

Her house, said his brain. And then some synapse misfired or failed to meet its rendezvous across some strange and nervous chasm and the boy's sense of where and when and now crumbled beneath him and he fell, down into the deep. Again, the knowledge, or perceived knowledge, *Her house*, but it was his mother's face, pale and pinched, that floated before him like a mirage.

I knew I could hunt her! he thought in triumph and laughed aloud, a coughing, barking sound tearing out of his throat and trailing in his wake as he sprinted across the front lawn, up the steps and turned the door handle.

She thought she could visit me, haunt me, and then hide. She doesn't know me. Her son.

He pushed into the cool dark.

Now she'll have to talk to me. I'll make her, I will. The scent that met his nose was unlike any that had ever lingered in his own home, the spice and tang of curry and vegetables and rice. But the boy's mind wrestled with the input, twisted into the cool cucumber smell of his mother's hands, the velvet wafting of bread and salt and yeast rising in the oven.

He stepped across plush shag carpet, only feeling linoleum through his soles, seeing the white expanse of his own kitchen at home rather than the dim hallway manned by a chocolate-colored grandfather clock.

I'll get my answers. And I won't have to wait until tonight. I'll find them here and now, here and now for sure. That's right, you can hide all you want but here I am, now, looking for you. I'm on to you and it won't matter where you go, I'll follow you and I will find you. That's right, that's right, make that a promise, my promise from me to you yeah me to you

The boy couldn't tell what was in his head from what was outside of it anymore and a rushing roaring growing building like the bed of pressure beneath a geyser waiting to blow to shoot its bubbles and burning and wet up and up in a gigantic spout and he didn't know if he was speaking with

133

tongue or mind but he thought the words might echo about him in the kitchen *hallway* kitchen and then it didn't matter, anyway, because he saw her, across the room *at the end of the hall* bright in the pouring of the sunlight in through the windows *dim and hesitating in the gathering gloom of the window-less way* and he stepped forward *he ran forward* feeling a smile melt across his lips, melting over his anger *a wide grimace peeling the pale lips apart* and the too-thin form turned *the stout frame turned* arms open in embrace *and ran* he stepped into the offering and *he flew in shrieking pursuit* he closed his eyes and sank in to her *a crack at his skull's base shooting fire bursts then throbbing black across his vision* cucumber scent filling his lungs *shag carpet infiltrates his nose where he crumples into oblivion* he is oblivious this is home —

34

DEE

The girl stood frozen and gray-faced just inside the open front door of her own home, the scene oozing into her brain. Don stood over his unconscious son, had gotten there ahead of her in his car, and now crumpled to the floor to gather the body of his child into his arms, weeping as he did so.

Her mother peeked from an open doorway at the opposite end of the hall, gray poof of hair vibrating over her fearful eyes, whites wide and glowing and afraid even from the interior distance. *She's never been afraid, not once in her whole life,* thought the girl and the hall lurched around her. Then her vision faded, thick and sticky shag carpet fibers her last knowledge before the floor rushed up and up to meet her own face in a velvet collision.

This place did not feel like home any more.

35

MIA'S JOURNAL

My belly still swells, as if it waits for the life that was taken from it. Empty cocoon wanting to cradle, nourish, bring forth something of itself that is not itself but something new, although not entirely, I think. I think it's my fault, the emptiness.

Don won't look at me. The nurses go about their business with the monitors and the screens and the tubes without speaking a word to me. They'll chat among themselves happily enough, though, if there's more than one of their pastel uniformed legion in the room at a time. And the doctor is no use, either. He just checks my chart, glances at me from the foot of this bed, and shakes his head a little as he scribbles notes and directions.

I can't ask. Or, more truly, I don't feel that I can ask. That I have the right. And I certainly do not have the nerve. Not if this is my fault, if I did it to me. To her. My daughter that will never be, now. But I can't imagine my sin, my wrong. I wish someone would tell me my mistake, and at the same time I shudder in fear at every footstep on the threshold and pray that I can remain in the unenlightened dark just a little longer. It is safer here. The truth is cold and made of metal, and it will cut me down if I know it.

The pain, the real pain in my flesh, my void abdomen, that is better now, less than it was although not completely gone. I don't know that it ever will be, not after this, after everything these four walls have seen. Isn't it strange that I miss the little person I never met, that I cursed upon first learning of? I cringed every time I saw in some mirror or window reflection how she swelled my belly, and now — now I just want her back, back in there. I don't care how huge I grow, how heavy or wide. I miss her. I miss my daughter.

What have I done? Again, again, I want to know and I cannot stand the thought of knowing. What a mess I am. I still smell the blood on the sheets, sticky, too cold for life, even though they have long been changed. My body is her tomb.

36

DON

The man's breath sounded too loud in his ears. It rushed in and out of him like a gale, echoing in the narrow hallway. He knew he should ask the woman shivering in the dim shadows if she was alright, or at least unhurt, to explain. But his vision was too full of his son's prone form, thin and pale and still as the dead the man buried, traded and bartered in. Don felt ill. The stench of some eastern dish cooking filled his nose, and his stomach heaved a little at the spice.

He swallowed, and then jumped at a tumbling thud from behind him. Turning, he saw the girl, the friend, on the ground. He stared, understanding escaping him.

"I — I'm sorry," he managed at last, not looking at the woman, presumably the girl's mother. "My son – he's . . . troubled. Sometimes." He paused. "The police are coming. I called them, before."

The woman came forward, and when she opened her mouth he braced, and instead flinched when only gentleness poured out. "We're newer in town, but I've heard about what happened to your wife. I'm so sorry. I can't imagine how hard it must be on a boy to lose his mother."

He opened his mouth, but no words came out, so he just nodded, feeling like a marionette.

She smiled a little as she passed to check on Dee. "There are no words for things like this."

No words for things like this. The two children's bodies spread out over the carpet, each a grim and distorted reflection of the other. And then his stomach heaved again, with greater purpose, and he stumbled outside and spilled his stomach's contents into the front yard's overgrown flowerbed.

THE CEMETERY

The cemetery waited, quiet and alone in the dimming sun. Row upon row of scattered dead laying in their places, hands folded in various states of decomposition, marked by granite and a gentle rise in the blanket green. Eras of dead, lives marching back to the advent of proclaimed civilization over the land, the sum of their accumulated years in the thousands, or higher. New headstones, small and sedate, brushed elbows with ornately carved angels and flourishes and graven fingers pointing to the sky, the heavens, eternity. The favored family plot aside, the cemetery was not divided into sections. There were no sects of religion or year of death or skin pigmentation. There were simply the dead, all favored or not in kind, equals in respect. The corpses held no enmity toward each other or their line of shepherds. This was the way, the way it always had been, always would.

Unless the way of things changed.

Unless, unless. The whisper, the wafting breath of a question hung in the highest limbs of the trees, snagged on the trimmed hedges, the carefully placed benches of wood and curling black iron. The graveyard seemed alive with the uncertainty. If there had been visitors that day (and there were none), they would not have been able to easily ignore the rising goose-pimples scaling their spines, the unnerving thought that something in the cemetery felt restless, churning with an energy that was just wrong, even unseemly, for the stately quiet of a resting place, a place that somehow existed both on the earth and some other plane. The visitors would not have stayed long.

But they would have been correct. Something stirred in the cemetery, or many somethings. Perhaps it was the souls of the dead, or perhaps the bodies they once inhabited and had since discarded. Perhaps the stones themselves vibrated and shook in the earth.

Whatever that strange something was, it knew, sensed a shift in the way of things, the way things always had been and always should be — but now, might not. Something had happened in the family of shepherds, and although the residents did not know what it could be and didn't much care, they felt it, knew it. The headstones and everything around them felt it. The trees and winding hedges and meticulously cropped grass and the benches and even the house, the office — they knew it, knew of a change, and trembled. Something had happened. The way could change, even today.

The cemetery waited in the dawning twilight and mourned the shift, the loss, the pallid collision of old with new as the first stars marked the blue expanse above.

38

MIA'S JOURNAL

Home again. Except it doesn't feel like home, or at least not the home that I left. Something is different, missing. It feels colder.

Of course, I suppose you could say that the missing element is obvious. The house, the cemetery, everything is mourning her loss, the loss of my first daughter. Miscarried.

What a strange word, miscarried. It implies such responsibility, that the mother (or really, the would-be mother, the would-have-been mother) committed some act of failure that caused her child's death, when really most miscarriages are due to biological, internal problems that she could hardly have known about, much less fixed. What an awful word, especially when it is spoken to you after the event, after you ruined your child's chance for life, after it was obviously all your fault even when it wasn't, when it couldn't be your fault at all.

Except in my case. In my case, with my child, I am very much at fault. The truth of this rests heavier on me with every day. I didn't believe it at first. But now, I think I begin to see my hand in this, my culpability. I wonder how I did not recognize it before.

The bald doctor delivered the news, finally. He stood at the foot of my hospital bed flanked by the two nurses and read statistics and test results from his clipboard and shook his head. Something about nutrition and minimum requirements, but my brain could not take in the man's words. There was no sense in them, not to me, not then or in that place.

I asked Don what the doctor meant after they left us alone to cry or fall into each other's arms or whatever it was that we were supposed to do. Don stood by the window, staring out — isn't it funny how, after all the time I spent in that room, I still don't know what that window looked out onto? — and told me that I had starved our baby to death. That I had nearly starved myself to death and should consider myself lucky to be alive at all. The word "lucky" seemed to stick in his throat, and I could see his jaw working as he tried not to cry. He held back the tears, but I could not. I am crying again now as I write these words.

I couldn't believe it at first. It seemed ridiculous. I didn't feel — don't feel — half starved. In fact, I still feel rather squashy despite having the life of my first child washed out of me in a scalding flood. But the nurses held a mirror up before my naked self and showed me how they could count my ribs, my vertebrae. They gave me brochures and pamphlets and newsletters decorated with cheerful rainbow food pyramids and filled with information about diet and caloric needs and body mass index statistics. They told me that I am EDNOS — eating disorder not otherwise specified. My relationship with food, my eating habits are "disordered." I am disordered.

Apparently I should not have been able to have gotten pregnant in the first place, that it was a miracle. It doesn't feel very miraculous to me. The nurses said that I need to gain ten to twenty pounds, to eat red meat and cheese and cashews and all other sorts of things that I trained myself to avoid as if they were marked by some exotic and virulent disease. The thought of eating a hamburger thick and bloody with ketchup and mayonnaise and fake, too-yellow mustard makes me taste vomit in my mouth even as I sit here in bed, far from food of any kind.

There I go again — I begin to catch myself, every now and again, thinking this way. "Disordered" thoughts, I suppose. I have to get used to that, to convince myself that this is wrong thinking. I begin to wonder how I am going to be beautiful to Don when I am no longer disordered, when I am fat. But maybe it won't matter as much. Maybe he is already too upset, to overwhelmed by disgust for even the thought of me that he will never look at me with husbandly lust in his eyes again, that he will never touch me or desire to touch and so I can eat spaghetti and meatballs and pie and all the chocolate in the world — chocolate! a bright flash in all this gloom. I haven't had chocolate in a half a lifetime, it feels — because now I am simply the housekeeper, the houseguest.

I feel ashamed when he comes in to bring me hot tea and honey and crackers with applesauce and I cannot meet his eyes with my own. How he must hate me. As he should. If only I had died and our daughter lived on together with her father, the two who deserve life without these tears, without my broken, disordered mind. Life fractures, doesn't it, just when everything feels rosy and right. Everything lies.

39

NAT

Nat thought they had buried him alive. He could almost remember it, the brush of the body bag against his nose as the paramedics zipped it closed, the trip by gurney and ambulance and gurney again to the morgue of the local hospital, examined by the coroner and then released to his father's professional and long-suffering custody, a gurney again back home, the final and forever home now, his shirt and shorts cut away by his father's icy scissors, the dry loneliness of embalming and then darkness, plush and sateen.

He moved his jaw against a tiny tickling at his chin. *Not dead, but buried,* he knew. He knew because he tried to scratch the itch but could not lift his hands. His feet refused to move in their proper range as well. Right hand and then left he tested, but each lifted only the tiniest bit before meeting resistance, so he knew that they had buried him and that death by suffocation or starvation or muffled and heart-bursting fear could not be far off. The boy didn't know which of the three was worse or better, but his heart had already set off for a breakneck gallop so he followed its lead and let the terrified bellow building at the bottom of his esophagus broil up and out into the coffin.

But the boy was still half unconscious and so what his mind intended for a scream came out as a thick and queasy moan. The slick horror of the sound existing in a manner it seemed it should have no right to adopt woke Nat fully and his eyes opened into slits and burning fluorescent flowed in and he realized that he was wrong, that he was not in his coffin, buried yet breathing, but that he must be in hell because he certainly had no claim on Heaven.

He thought it a little strange that hell resembled a hospital. Blinking and flinching a little against the brightness after the deep and colorless dark of unconsciousness, he took in the textured teal wall paper, the matching tiled floor, the whirr and hum of machinery and monitors next to his head, although they remained out of his vision's scope.

The boy's chin continued itched, and as it was increasingly obvious that his father had not allowed him to go into the ground alive — although Nat still felt a little fuzzy as to if he was alive in a hospital or dead in one — he lifted his left hand to scratch the spot. Something rattled a little and his hand stopped before it reached its destination. Feeling the insides of his lids sliding against his eyeballs like rasping sandpaper, Nat looked down and down his body, thin frame barely raising a mound beneath the standard issue blankets. There, snaking about his wrists, still pale despite a summer spent in the outdoors of the cemetery, spread two padded bracelets. *No, not bracelets*, he saw, tugging upwards against the fawn-colored padding, *restraints*. He had seen them on a television show once, something about a man who heard, who listened to invisible voices in his head telling him to hurt people, to kill them, even. The man died when one of his intended victims shot him in the temple with her husband's hunting rifle.

Nat's stomach felt as if it were suddenly filled with ice cubes, bloated and colder than the dead his father stored in the workroom freezers. *I'm going to die*, he thought, tugging at the restraints. *I'm going to hear the voices and someone's going to kill me.* He wondered who would be the one to commit the act. His father?

His father. The boy blinked. *Where's my dad?* He felt very young all of a sudden. And then, "Where's my dad?"

The words spread into the room, thin and pale, and Nat shivered a little. He wiggled his torso, trying to tuck deeper under the scratchy warmth of the blankets, and the back of his skull seemed to split open with an electric storm of pain that blew his vision out into the glare of white heat. He stopped moving and lay panting, feeling the unyielding foam of the hospital mattress beneath his backbone.

The boy gritted his jaw, the pain rolling away a little at a time. After what seemed a long while, the shocks were gone and his brain felt like his own again. He moved to get out of bed, to explore the floor and find someone who could tell him where his dad was, why he was in a hospital in the first place. But there came that tinny jingling from his wrists and ankles again and he fell back against the pillows. He had forgotten the shackles.

He had not, however, forgotten hospitals. The endless sitting and waiting, the mingling smells of mass-produced cafeteria food and human sweat, the burning of ammonia at the back of his throat after he breathed the air for too long. No, all that was still far too familiar. He and his father had spent hours at her bedside, staring at the skeletal form that wasted closer to death every day, and even Nat could see her fresh descent into gray-skinned death with every visit. The boy would press in close to his father, trembling at the leering mask his mother's face had pulled back into. But his father would only squeeze his shoulder and press him closer to that terrible vision and his blood would run cold at her touch even while his stomach flooded with boiling shame.

So he knew what the cord that wound down the mattress from somewhere behind the head of the bed to end in a knobbly button was for, and how to use it. He reached for the intercom button, but even that lay just out of reach. Sighing, he yanked at the restraints and then let his arms lay at his sides again.

What did I do to earn these? he wondered, glaring at the padded cuffs. *Was I scratching at my stitches in my sleep or something?* If he even had stitches, of course. He realized with a slight shock that he still didn't even know what was wrong with him, what was wrong in his body. Something in his head, judging from the pain that had detonated there earlier. But aside from that, he sensed nothing.

And where is my dad? He wanted answers, he wanted to scratch his chin, but mostly he just didn't want to be alone. Not in the hospital. *Do I look like she looked yet? Is that what places like these to do you?* A chilly trail of goosebumps crept up his arms.

A rustle outside the door and a nurse breezed in, dressed in warm pink scrubs. Nat thought that the curvy woman looked like the type who would give very satisfying hugs. Then he though that he would really like to be hugged, and had to blink furiously to keep the tears that filled his eyes from spilling down his cheeks.

"Oh, hello there!" the woman said, smile broad on her gray hair-framed face. "Can't say I expected you to be awake yet. How are you feeling, hon?"

"Where's my dad?" The words left his tongue too quickly, and he felt as if he were throwing them at her. "He's tall, and he's got black hair — black and gray, really — and his name is Don."

The smile dimmed a little in sympathy. "Yes, I know who your father is. But he's just stepped out for a few minutes. I told him to, you can't stay cooped up in here forever. So I sent him on down to the cafeteria for a cup of coffee and told him to stick his head outside for a few minutes, breathe some fresh air."

"He's here? In the hospital?"

The woman nodded. "Or somewhere very close by, at least."

The boy sank back deeper into his pillows and exchanged his lungs of old air for fresh oxygen. *I'm not alone,* his brain shouted, so loud that it seemed to affect how well he could hear the beeps from his monitors, the passion shuffle and voices in the hallway. *I'm not alone! Dad's here.*

The nurse checked the chart hanging off of the bed's foot-board, making a few notes with a pen before bustling to stand at his head. As he watched, she read information unin-telligible to him from the monitor and pressed some buttons there with her clean and manicured fingers and jotting notes onto the clipboard. He found himself wanting a hug from her once again.

"It's your turn now, dear," she said, turning to face him, green eyes warm when they met his gaze. "How are you feeling? Any pain or queasiness?"

He stopped himself from nodding just in time, and swallowed the heat that flared up at the back of his skull. "My head hurts, when I move it." She noted that on his chart, purple pen ducking and weaving across. "Why do I have to wear these things?" The chains of the cuffs jingled as he lifted both arms.

"They are just to make sure that you don't hurt yourself."

"But why? Why would you worry about that? What happened?"

The woman sucked in her cheeks for a moment. "Your father will be back in soon enough, hon. I'll let him explain."

"Well, could you take them off, these chains? I can't even scratch my chin." Then, as an afterthought, "It itches."

"I'm sorry, but we're going to have to leave them on for the time being. The doctor might want to stop in and check up on you first, just to make sure it's all clear."

"Make sure *what's* all clear?" Her words buzzed around inside his brain and he struggled to pin their sense to his own understanding, but failed.

She patted his knee as she went to hang his chart back in it's place. "Your father will tell you everything, I'm sure of it. Just lay back and rest now, okay? It'll make you feel better. And I'll have one of the food service folks bring you something to eat in a little bit. Sound good?"

It didn't sound all that good to Nat, but she had already whisked out the door and he lay there, still restrained and more confused than before, and very much alone. He sighed.

40

DON

Don found it hard to believe that the sun shone with such zeal down into the hospital courtyard, that the world had not turned as cold and shriveled as his own insides felt. *But then,* he thought, *that's always been the way of the weather. It refuses to give you a nice, weepy day when all you want is for all the world to cry along with you. It smiles at your pain.*

He glared up at the blue sky, cloudless and that warm velvet of early autumn afternoons, and sipped at his coffee. Typical of hospital bulk brewed caffeine, it flowed over his tongue too black and too hot, but he swallowed anyway, enjoying how it scalded the roof of his mouth, the passage of his esophagus, how they would be raw by the bottom of the paper cup. Already he could feel how his sense of taste numbed from the acrid liquid and took another mouthful.

The walls of the medical complex rose tall and purposeful around the square courtyard that was lined with benches and non-native foliage, all circling a tiny central fountain in which a few massive goldfish wandered. The few other people outside did not look at Don or meet his eyes, but he didn't mind. That was just the way of hospitals, everyone caught up in their own tragedies, their own waiting and waiting and waiting.

A man in a wheelchair with red weals sweeping down his face and neck, reappearing to lace across his arms, sat smoking a cigarette. The cloud of smoke seemed to condense around him and yet somehow permeate the entire courtyard with its thick and smothering stench. Don breathed it in, gritting his teeth against it at first, and then inhaling it in great gulps, feeling the nicotine ease into his heart and mind and soothe the heat of their worry.

Don drained the last of the coffee from his cup, watching how the few black bean pockmarks pooled in the final drips that refused to flow to the call of gravity but suspended from the upturned paper bottom. He crumpled the stiff white vessel and threw it in the trash can as he turned and stepped back through the automatic doors into the hospital atmosphere, somehow so much more oppressive than the second hand exhaust from even an army of smokers. He ground his teeth together against the chill that snuck down his back and made the winding journey past half-distributed stacks of patient lunches and the nurses' stations – *Always busy and bustling until you needed a nurse*, he thought – up to his son's room. The man paused for a moment outside the door, swallowed once, twice, and then stiffened his shoulders as he entered, stiffening against the expected sight of his son's pale form draped across the bed.

He blinked. The boy's face looked back at him, eyes open – *Open! And alive!* – and full of gathering questions. He saw how Nat's thin face relaxed a little as he came into the room and had to swallow again against the bile that threatened to rise.

Don't look at me like that, he pleaded, *not when I'm the one who put you here.*

He cleared his throat as he crossed the space from door to bedside in two smooth strides and brushed the hair back from Nat's forehead with a careful palm. "Hey there, son."

"Hey." The young voice filtered into Don's hearing as if it traveled a long way to reach the room.

"How are you feeling?"

A pause. "I don't know. My head. It hurts when I move. Okay, though, besides that." The words slurred together and the man wondered what kind of drugs the intravenous tubes were feeding his son, if any at all.

"That's good." Don winced at his own words. *Good? What is good about any of this?* "You hit your head.

"Dad," said Nat, and now every muscle in the man's body tensed, because he knew was coming next, "Dad, what happened? Why am I here?"

Another swallow. "Well," he began. "You – something happened – you went a little nuts for a while there." He swallowed again, or tried, but just choked a little on the workings of his over-dry esophagus.

The boy stared, and the crimson trails in his bloodshot eyes stood out thick and bold. Don supposed that would be a side-effect of being cracked across the skull. *What is the good here?* he asked himself again.

"Nuts?" asked Nat.

His father nodded. "Yes. Like you used to get before, after mom — died." He felt his own neck grow hot at the word even while he watched what little color remained in Nat's cheeks drain away. "Do you remember anything? Any of what happened?"

The boy thought for a moment. "No. Not really."

Of course not. Don turned, slid the chair where he had sat sentinel over his unconscious son before stealing a few moments alone with his coffee close to the bedside, and settled into it. "Then," he said, heaving a sigh, "let me tell you."

So he forced his brain to march back and wade through memories of heat and panic and weave together the thread of what happened, or what he knew of what happened, from the first pounding of the boy's feet up from the graveyard into Don's surprised arms, to the girl and the police and then the horrible chase, steering his car down the street and screeching to a halt beside the blue house where the door hung open and the lawn ornamentation lay broken and scattered, where he knew somehow *somehow* his son would be and throwing the car into park even while he launched himself from the vehicle and into the stranger's home, where he saw Nat, heard him raging at the woman at the end of the hall, and then how he'd passed out.

Low blood sugar, doctor had said. Don had wanted to rage himself, rage at the doctor when she'd said that, at how much it reminded him of what happened to Mia, but he didn't.

Silence hung over the pair. Then a tiny jangle as Nat shifted his feet beneath the blankets.

"I — we — there was a ghost," Nat said, avoiding his father's gaze.

Don frowned at the unexpected word. "A ghost?"

"In one of Dee's photographs . . ." The boy's voice trailed away as his eyes flew open wide. "Dee! Is she okay? I remember, I yelled at her."

"She's fine. She fainted, too. She's already been discharged."

"Dee was here." Nat's words were not a question.

"Yes, the paramedics took her in to the hospital, too. But she was just scared, and she's going just fine." The same ambulance that had brought Nat to this hospital had also brought the girl, already stirring out of her collapse, with her mother. Don's ride with them to the hospital had been silent and cold but for the working of the paramedics. He could not meet the woman's eyes, even as he felt her gaze searching for his own.

Don rubbed the heels of his palms into his eye sockets. "It just happened so fast."

"Dad?" This time Nat's voice was quiet, afraid. "Am I broken?"

The man felt his forehead begin to crumple as the words shred into his heart, but he forced his face into what he hoped was a genuinely reassuring expression. "No more than anyone else would be by what you've been through, son."

Nat's lips twisted. "I don't believe you. You should lock me up. I'm too messed up, too weird to be around people."

Don hesitated, breath catching in his throat. The doctor had suggested considering hospitalizing the boy in an in-patient mental health therapy program. To help him along on his healing journey, she'd said, not unkindly. The thought made Don feel like he'd been losing a son along with the wife that was already gone. *But then, maybe Nat is already gone, too, and the only way of getting him back is to give him away*, he thought.

He shook his head. "Nat," he said, shoving his thoughts aside, "you are broken. You're hurting, very badly. There's a big difference."

"If that's true, then why am I wearing these?" Nat lifting his hands, offering the restraints encircling his wrists.

"To help you," Don said, but even he didn't believe his own reedy words. And then tears rolled against his cheeks, and they seemed somehow cold and sandpapery against his face.

The boy closed his eyes. "You can't help me. No one can. No one should want to."

"I want to." Don's voice emerged as the barest raw whisper.

Nat's eyes snapped open, narrowed and unsure. "Why?"

The man blinked. "Because you're my son. Because I love you and would do anything for you, Nat. Anything."

"How can you love this?" murmured Nat, eyes closing again, head turning away. "How could anyone." It was not a question.

The two sat. Soon Nat's breathing evened and lengthened, and Don knew that sleep had fallen over his son once more, leaving him alone with his own coughing, guttural sobs that crashed silently through him.

41

MIA'S JOURNAL

Don made me dinner this evening. Pumpkin gnocchi. I was quite surprised when he pushed into the room with a tray laden with steaming plates of the pasta and sparkling cider.

"I would have brought wine," he said as he set the tray on the night-stand, "except I don't think that would go well with your medication."

Probably not, although now I cannot get the yearning for a glass of red wine, smooth and dark and regal, out of my head. It's the power of suggestion at work, I suppose. I normally don't even like red wine, or really any wine at all. For us, alcohol is for celebrations.

Which makes me wonder if Don is celebrating. What on this earth could make him think that we have anything to celebrate now? We just lost a baby – I lost it for us, really, killed it. And now I feel so tired, so empty that I can barely sit up in bed and read or crochet most days, much less get up and live truly. All the cleaning and cooking falls to Don now. He must hate me, hate the burden I have become to him. How could anyone love this?

The pumpkin gnocchi tasted good. I didn't know that Don had such a talent in the kitchen. Although he used to make me pancakes, and those were always wonderful. Gnocchi seems a step up, though. He sat with me in bed and we ate the little orange balls of dough and I felt warm and well taken care of.

And, the biggest surprise of all, I felt full – and I didn't hate it. I didn't want to run to the bathroom (well, in theory – I don't think I'll be running much at all any time in the close future) and heave my stomach's contents into the toilet basin. I didn't writhe away from my husband's touch as he stroked my belly after our plates lay, abandoned and empty, on the tray next to the drained cider glasses. I didn't feel heavy or bloated and repulsive, and I can't imagine why.

But I won't argue, cannot allow myself any complaint. It is heaven, or a piece of it, to be able to eat and enjoy and digest and love like this. And I will be well and strong again, someday, and perhaps we will have another child and I can be a better mother, a real one and have a real try at it and maybe, just maybe, Don will forgive me and I will have redeemed myself in his eyes.

The gnocchi sours a little in my stomach at this thought, that I have turned myself into the filthy, the unlovable. But that will change. It must. When I can get out of this bed, I will be — I vow it, I suppose, in this bed, in this moment — I will be the wife he needs, he deserves, poor man, and I will be strong and beautiful and so one day when he looks at me, he will not see the spectral shadow of the daughter I murdered. That is all I can see when I fix my hair in the handheld mirror on my bedside stand, so I know he must, too. And how could he love that?

NAT

Nat let the oppressive yet somehow comfortable heat of the car soak into him as they drove away from the hospital and back to the cemetery. Back home, where it would be just him and his father and the dead, the dead always watching and listening.

And the ghosts, what about them? Will they be there, waiting, too? Or did they ever exist at all? he wondered, the gentle rumble of the sedan lulling him into a half-sleep. He thought of his mother, and then tried to think of nothing at all.

When he woke up in the hospital that morning, the nurse told him that he would be going home that day. His father had to take care of some paperwork before they could go. The boy later heard words like "social worker" and "complicated grief" and "cognitive behavioral therapy" passing amongst the nursing staff, words that turned his core to slush. He had dozed, then, forced himself into unconsciousness, and when he woke to the drone of a conversation between his father and another person – *The social worker,* he thought, *come to rescue my dad, to take me away from him* – he did not allow his ears to take in their dialogue, refused himself comprehension.

Instead, he lay there, restraints now removed, and imagined what the foster home might be like, and the new family he would eventually find himself injected into, expected to assimilate and forget all about Nat, the Nat of the cemetery, Nat the youngest son in a lineage of morticians. That Nat would have to disappear, or he'd find himself with no family at all, just a string of extended foster care stays. He knew all this because some official or other had discussed the intricacies of child custody with him after his mother died, and while he'd barely understood half of what the brown-suited man told him, but managed well enough to know that the government would not take as good care of him as his father, even if the man hated him now, didn't want to look at him ever again. Besides, Nat would miss the graveyard.

So it was with some surprise that he found himself dressing in a new change of clothes that his father brought for him and following the tall man out of the room. *Weird how I only get to see what the hospital is like now that I'm leaving it*, he considered on the journey out of the hospital and into the car, bound for home.

The two figures in the car exchanged no words on the drive. Nat didn't mind, really. It felt easier, and he didn't want to make his father talk to him unless the man wanted to. So they drove in silence. *This is better*, the boy told himself, and wished he didn't feel so disappointed that his dad said nothing, offered him nothing. He closed his eyes and let the sun warm his face.

Even with his eyes closed, he knew when they reached the cemetery. The quiet trundle of the car before turning left into the drove with that precise bump of the curb pressing into each tire, the right-hand easing as his father steered the car up through the ranks of granite stones, up and up, past the office and then the engine coming to rest at last in the garage.

Nat opened his eyes, but did not move even when his father unbuckled his own seatbelt and left the sedan, moving to remove something from the trunk. Once he got out of the car, he would have to go somewhere else, find something to do with himself, and he could not bring himself to think of anything that he wanted to do. And there would be, some-time, words with his father, and that knowledge made his muscles ache, too, until all he wanted to do was fall into bed and sleep until he grew a beard and the beard, tangled and winding about the foot of the bed, turned gray, then white, and he died, old and peaceful and asleep as breath left him.

In the side view mirror he could see his father coming around to his door, so the boy forced his fingers to fumble at the seat belt buckle, depressing its clasp and ready to swing his feet to the cement floor of the garage when the man swung the door open. He saw his old clothes, dirty and stained with splotches of rust and brown in places, crumpled under his father's arm. The sight of the bloodstains from when he'd his head made his stomach leap and he dropped his eyes to his unlacing sneakers.

The hand on his shoulder startled Nat. He flinched and the hand disappeared.

"Are you okay?" asked his father.

He shrugged. *I don't know*, he thought. *How can I?* The boy thought again of his mother and swallowed hard.

"Let's go inside." Still looking at the floor, Nat followed his father's loafer-shod feet up the stairs into the house, keeping

161

time with those seemingly vast shoes until he found himself at a standstill in the kitchen.

"Are you hungry? I can make you something."

A long pause. Nat fiddled with the hem of his shirt. At the mention of food, he realized that his limbs felt weak and wiggly with hunger, but he hated to take anything from this man, to ask for anything. *I've already been enough trouble*, the boy thought.

"Come on, son," his father encouraged, stepping over to the refrigerator. Nat glanced up to see the man standing with his hand on the fridge's door handle, attempting a little grin, the bundle of ruined clothing gone. "You name it, I'll make it. If we have all the ingredients, of course. I haven't done the grocery shopping yet this week, so we're a little low on a few things." *My fault again.* "But I'm sure we've got the makings of something you'd like."

"It's okay," Nat said, hating how the words slurred together, his tongue thick with disuse. "I'll eat whatever you make."

He felt his father's eyes on his face, and then the heat of blood rushing into his cheeks. He could never keep his cool when he needed to. "This is your day, son. Your homecoming. I want to make something special for you. If you're hungry."

Homecoming? Is that what this is? The word sounded too grand for the actual event, as if some sort of celebration should be involved. "I'm hungry. I could eat."

"Good!" The boy heard the faint shrill of desperation at the edge of the man's voice. "Good. So what do you feel like?"

Nat thought the man was trying too hard. He wanted to go back to the stiff velvet silence of the car, but his father seemed determined to not let him alone. *So I guess we're having the words now,* he decided. *Or at least some words.*

"Spaghetti," the boy said aloud. "Do we have that?"

His father nodded. "You bet we do. Tomato sauce and meatballs with that?"

"Yeah. Meatballs are good. And parm, if there's any."

The man clanged about the kitchen, pulling pots and spoons and bowls from closets, plunking a massive box of pasta down on the counter. "Parmesan cheese? I'm pretty sure we have that, too."

Now a pot of water sat working its way into a boil on the stovetop while his father poured tomato sauce into a little pan and began to chop up a handful of mushrooms, throwing the pieces into the heating sauce. *He's never put mushrooms in the sauce before.* Nat sensed that this meal would end up being a lot fancier than he had intended, or wanted. *I don't even like mushrooms.* And then he realized he had no right to dislike anything his father made, not after the hospital and his episode, as one of the nurses had called it. So he sank into a chair at the kitchen table and watched his father bustle along the counter and, after steaming bowls of tomato-drenched pasta sat before the pair and the man led them in thanks, Nat chewed and swallowed every mushroom without complaint, enjoying how their spongy texture turned his guilty stomach.

The boy's room opened its door to a stranger. At least, he felt like a stranger to its blue-painted senses. The Nat who had last tied his sneakers on the center of its woven rug of spiraling colors, the boy whom the bed had held as he shivered through nights and nightmares, who had wept at death and smiled into books in the day and who wrote in the beaten spiral notebook – that boy was gone.

They took care of each other, in a way, the room and the boy. Nat dusted the sagging shelves of the two bookcases that stood, one perpendicular to the other, in a corner next to the door, and he smoothed the sheets of the twin bed with gentle fingers and made sure that most of his socks and underwear and ink-stained shirts made their way into the hamper hiding in the closet. In its turn, the room kept in the heat that should have seeped out through drafts around the single window pane, through the creaking floor boards, and made the last glimmers of evening sunlight linger a little longer in the corners.

The boy that lay on the bed, rigid and pale faced, did not seem the type to tend the room, to care about it or even consider it at all. The room felt how this new Nat's attention turned inward more than before, although toward what it did not know. His heart, perhaps, or those strangely shaped stomachs that all humans have, or maybe his lymph nodes. The room did not know, but the floor boards creaked especially loudly through that first night as it trembled while the boy lay atop the covers in his clothes, sneakers and all, staring up at its white ceiling until, finally, he fell into a pallid and shallow sleep.

43

MIA'S JOURNAL

I woke up this morning and felt ponderous, just absolutely heavy. For the first time since the miscarriage, I looked down at my length of skin and skeleton, naked in under the shower's streaming faucet, and felt vast. I don't know what it is about today, or about me or what I ate yesterday night (eggplant parmesan, incidentally) or what I dreamed of in the night, but suddenly my own flesh feels too tight for the bulk that is me.

The scale does not help me feel any more or less insane. It tells me that I am one pound heavier, on average, than when I came home one and a half weeks ago. The unwell and inflamed part of me that sends me to the toilet with a finger down my throat, retching all the way, is pleased at that result. But then the sane portion of my brain can't help but wonder, why, an eternity of why's, do I feel this way? I have no answer to give it. One pound wouldn't, could never, account for the weight I feel dragging at every joint, every follicle, pulling me down and down and down again into the dirt. This body will bury me.

So I must try to ignore it, this ludicrous and unexplained ponderosity. I don't know what more I can do. Especially since I promised — no, I vowed, on pages exactly like these — I vowed to become healthy, to do better by my husband, to give life again, God willing. And now I add something to that vow. I vow to live according to God's vision of beauty instead of my own, instead of the world's. "Beauty is fleeting," the proverb says, but a woman who fears God is valuable, has worth to him, to others, and perhaps even — or should I say especially? I wonder — to herself.

I want to have worth, to be a worthwhile person. But I'm not sure I can be that or do that or even hope for something that wonderful if I try to build that value on my face, my body alone. In fact, I know I can't. Image isn't everything, or so one of the nurses muttered under her breath while she tended my monitor at the hospital, thinking me asleep. But I wasn't, and I heard her and hated her for it. Now, though . . . I think there is a great wisdom in her words, regardless of what she meant when she created them.

Don is calling up the stairs that breakfast is ready. He had designs on making omelettes and green beans, wonderful man, or so he told me before he headed down to prepare the food, leaving me to shower. I can't imagine what I've done to deserve him, to earn the presence of anyone even slightly resembling him in my life. He deserves someone more than myself, I know that much, and I am thankful that he's mine. Painfully thankful, even, without reservation, panting with the weight of gratitude on my heart that has nothing to do with how wide my thighs might feel.

I love him, my husband. I am in love with him. And, the biggest wonder of all, he loves me, I think, in spite of everything.

44

DON

Don sat in the sunlight that pooled over her grave, her words open across his lap. He did not know why he continued to return to her journals again and again. What he found there would never change, and never could. The same struggles and tears and traitorous glimmers of hope before the empty pages that stretched on into eternity.

Did you know? he asked the silent face of granite. *Did you know how much I cared for you, how you were the center of everything for me? Even when you were sick, you were wonderful. You are wonderful in memory. I miss you. And I love you still.*

The stone seemed to laugh in mute reply. Even in death he felt her disbelief. He could almost hear her words, "How could you love this, love me?"

It's simple. It is now, just as it was then, when I could still hold you and touch your hair. You were my wife. You are my wife and that makes you everything. Your heart and mind are better than any I've known, and while you were beautiful, too, the rest is nothing, just the icing, and you can't have good icing without good cake.

A whisper of air parting above. He glanced up to see a crow flying over, black against the deep blue of summer's sky. The man followed its path with his eyes until it became obscured by trees.

His fingers moved against the journal. The marker was just a mass of rock, silent and solid until forever. He felt silly having a conversation with it, as if it was her. But wasn't it worse than suppressing the thoughts, and the grief? That's what Nat's doctor at the hospital had said. Complicated grief.

There had been no sign of the boy yet that morning. After dinner the previous night, Nat had simply crept up to his room and shut the door. Don himself had slept fitfully, waking with a start at every creak and settling of the house, every indistinct noise sounding through the darkness that was made that much more awful by the night's slow churning, on and on through the smallest hours.

He hoped that Nat managed to get more sleep than he did. *He needs to rest, I think, to get his feet back under him. And his heart, maybe.* The man glared at the placid face of the stone now.

It was him you hurt the most when you left. I can handle it, although it's the hardest thing I've ever had to bear. But he's just a kid, and he needs you. He needs his mother, and you went and died for some stupid cause.

He waited, as if to see if he'd be caught out, called on his anger. But the etched letters did not shift into even the slightest slant of remorse. The doctor had also said that healthy expression of anger was a normal and healthy part of grieving. It felt both good and terrible.

With a sigh, he snapped the journal shut, tossing it to the ray-warmed grass. He lay back, groaning a little along with his complaining spine. It had been a long while since he had done this, lay in the quiet calm of his inherited way of life, and already he could feel the cemetery's unrocked serenity seeping from the earth into his ribs, his legs and shoulders, cool strength girding itself about him.

We'll be okay. The flash of insight came to him as if the fact was already true. *It might take a long while, but we'll make it through, Nat and I. We'll be okay.* He closed his eyes and smiled at the stars that hid, modest and bashful, behind the cerulean day-bright canopy of sky.

MIA'S JOURNAL

Church, Sunday morning. Is writing poetry during the sermon a sin? It is my offering on this new day, this time set aside for praise and glory to God. I feel strong here, close to the others who stumble along in their faith, and I feel God hears my troubles, knows them, has carried them himself instead of sending some lackey angel to shoulder the burden. Amazing. Sometimes, many times, I don't feel the Word living in my heart, I just know it. But now, today as I sit and let the worship music bleed into me, sunlight from the window warming me on one side while Don's frame settles me on the other, now I feel it tremendously. I feel lucky.

Sanctuary stands

about the gathering

stamping snow over holy

threshold, stepping

into handshakes, warm

and broken hearts alike

filter to audience

Sentinel upholstered silver

and the unseen host raises

swords and praise with the mortal

voices, vibrating skins

and strings gifted

to the King

Vines tendril my heart, guilt

dismissed by made-man sweat,

I think I am becoming

free

4 6

NAT

The door to Nat's bedroom swung inward.

"No, thanks," he mumbled from where he lay on the bed, face pressed down into the pillow. He liked how the breath hissed in just that soft way as the cotton case impeded the air's travel. The words seemed to buzz into the fabric and fill it. They felt almost thick enough to take a bit of, to chew on, the boy thought.

"What are you talking about?"

He jerked in surprise, then rolled over. The room seemed over-bright after his imposed darkness, and he squinted to see Dee standing in the doorway.

"Hey," he said.

She smirked. "Hey, yourself. What did you mean, 'No thanks'? That makes no sense."

"Um," began Nat, and his voice felt gravelly from lack of use as it rolled up from his throat. "I thought you were my dad.

He keeps wanting me to do stuff. But I don't want to do any of it."

"Like what kind of stuff?"

"Oh. Just things." His brain refused to offer a good example. "Like going for a walk, I guess, or reading."

"Why don't you want to do any of those things?"

He heaved himself up, swinging his legs over the side of the bed so that he sat upon its edge. "I don't know. I'd just rather not."

"Are you mad at him?"

"My dad?"

The girl nodded. Her red curls bounced about her shoulders, and with a pang in his belly Nat realized that he had missed that sight, had missed his friend.

He thought for a moment. "I don't know. Maybe. I don't know."

"That's okay." She leaned against the doorframe. "So what *have* you been up to this whole time, then?"

"Well, I was in the hospital for a few days."

"Me, too. I mean, not for a few days. They just sent me to the hospital, too, just in case."

"Are you okay?" *Did you go crazy with me?*

She made a face. "I just passed out, nothing serious. I probably didn't even have to go, but I think it made my mom feel better."

"Your mom," Nat murmured, more to himself than to his friend. "Is – um, is she okay, too?"

Dee's raspberry lips turned down at the corners a little. "She's freaked out, I guess. At least, she was." A pause. "Do you want to come over?"

He blinked. "What? Right now?"

The girl shrugged. "Yes, pretty much."

"I don't know." Nat swallowed, hard. "I'd rather stay here."

"And do what? Sleep? Do nothing? Because that's kind of what it seems like you've been doing for the past week." She had her fists planted on her hips now.

"But — your mom. Won't she, uh, not want me at your house? After – everything?"

"Oh." She rolled her eyes. "I forgot. She's the one who told me to ask."

The boy stared across the room, feeling his chin begin to dangle a little. It didn't seem possible that there could be any scrap of truth to Dee's words. "*Why?*"

"We're making cookies. Peanut butter chocolate chip," she said, as if that explained everything.

"Cookies."

"They're really tasty, I promise." Now her words whined with wheedling. "Come on, Nat, don't be silly. What happened is over with, so come *on* already."

He gripped at the edge of the mattress until his knuckles turned white. "I don't want to."

"Because you're scared."

"No." The word erupted from the boy's lips too fast, too forcefully to feel truthful. "Because – because I just shouldn't. Okay?"

She shook her head. "Nope, it's not okay."

Nat glared at her. "Well, I'm not going with you. I don't want cookies."

"Then I'm not leaving. Not without you." Her chin stuck forward, and Nat suddenly felt very tired.

"How long do I have to stay? If I go at all, I mean."

The girl raised an eyebrow, and he knew that the battle was won, and not by him. "Long enough for cookies."

With a sigh, he slid off the bed. "Let's go, then." *Might as well get it over with fast, like taking a band-aid off,* he thought, or hoped. He was not sure which.

She flashed a wide grin at him, and another pang of wistful melancholy hit him as he realized how much that sight meant to him. "I knew you'd end up coming over," she said with satisfaction as they cascaded down the steps. They paused in the kitchen long enough for Nat to write a note to his dad, then headed out of the house, which felt suddenly less oceanic to Nat than when he had first arrived home, helpless and adrift in its emptiness.

"Smarty pants," and to Nat's surprise he felt a smile tickle the corner of his own mouth.

She laughed. "I missed you."

"Hey." The boy ground to a halt among the gravestones. "I'm sorry. About everything."

With a shrug, she said, "I know." Dee seemed like she meant it. And, what was more, he believed her.

Nat trembled with every step of their journey. But he let Dee lead him on, up the front steps of the too-blue house, and into the kitchen. He swallowed as they stepped over the room's threshold.

It was not a small room, and every wall was lined with chipped formica counters except for the corner which had a table tucked into it, four painted yellow chairs crowding around it. And over the counters and the table top spread a host of seemingly random items. Paint brushes stood in cups of water, lay scattered next to stacks of new and used paper and parchment and thin store-bought canvases. Half-kneaded lumps of clay crowded against philosophy books and interior decorating magazines and newspapers whose yellowing pages, Nat saw at a second glance, were dated from the previous week. In between the ranging chaos, to which the boy felt there was some system of organization that he failed to grasp, but only just, huddled opened bags of flour and sugar and a partially melted stick of butter and a vast bowl filled with the stubbly brown of a multitude of chocolate chips and open recipe books, pages thumbed into dullness from much turning. Over one of these books stood a woman, tracing down a page with a trailing finger. As Nat followed his friend into the kitchen, the woman looked up.

"Well, now," she said, gray-green eyes peering through fuschia-rimmed glasses to look him up and down, "you don't look so very ferocious, do you?"

"Um," he said, and certainly felt anything but ferocious. The woman's moderate girth, thick gray curls streaked black and gray but otherwise very much like her daughter's crimson locks, her freckled cheeks all chimed some chord in Nat's memory. *From what happened, when I was here,* he thought, *That's why she looks familiar.* But he still could not remember the actual incident, and was not sure that he wanted to, or even wanted to try.

"Don't just stand there," she ushered them in, fluttering her strong-looking hands, "come on in, find a place to sit or squat or do whatever you like. Don't be afraid to move things."

"I'm afraid to move stuff," said Dee, sticking her tongue out at her mother. "You never know what's buried around here."

"As long as it's not dead, there's nothing to worry about," muttered the woman.

"Dead?" The question was out of his mouth before he had a chance to bite it back.

"We found a dead mouse in the stove once," said Dee. "It smelled kind of bad for days before we discovered it. But we hardly ever use the oven, so no one thought to look in there."

The woman made a show of shuddering, winking at Nat as she did so. "I do like a good mess, as long as it doesn't involve any carcasses." She paused. "Oh, and you should call me Helena."

"Oh," he said. "Okay." Then, feeling that he should offer something to the conversation, "My dad's a mortician."

"I know it," nodded Helena. "A noble art, to be sure. For those that can do it. Like I said, I can't abide carcasses."

"They're not so bad," said Nat. "They don't do much."

Dee gave a short laugh, revealing a mouthful of half-masticated chocolate chips melting across her tongue. "I hope not! That would be awful, to have to live with zombies."

"Or ghosts," Nat said, more to himself than to the two females. He had forgotten about his ghosts, at least for a little while, but now the nightmares and the dark hours filled with trembling and cold sweat returned to his memory and shivered at the thought of going back to that.

"It sounds like there's a story there," said the older woman, raising her eyebrows.

He shrugged. "I don't know," he mumbled, feeling the tips of his ears grow warm. "There are no such things as ghosts —"

A exasperated explosion of air burst from Dee. "Don't start all that again," she said, swallowing the last of the chips. "Even if he won't admit it, I think that there are some ghosts in the cemetery. And some of them, or one, at least, might be haunting Nat. Remember the photograph I showed you? That's our evidence."

"Hmm," said her mother. "I do remember. And a cemetery does seem a logical place to find ghosts."

"I think," said the boy, choosing his words with care, "I think it might be my mother."

"What makes you think that?" Helena asked.

"Because I saw her — or I thought I did, anyway — in my room one night, and then Dee took that picture, and — I don't know, I just have a feeling." The heat from his ears spread down to his cheeks, and he stared down at his beaten sneakers, afraid to look at Helena's face, afraid that her face would be painted over with mockery, that she would laugh at him. *Ghosts don't exist, and even if they did, adults never believe in that sort of thing,* Nat thought and waited for her to tell him that he was being ridiculous, that he should get on with it and grow up, already.

"Hmm," she said instead.

"What?" said Dee with raised eyebrows. "Just 'hmm'?"

"Yes," said her mother, frowning a little, eyes sparkling. "Just that."

"You . . . don't think I'm crazy?" Nat asked, half afraid to hear her answer.

"Well, that's a bit of a tricky question. You did come into my house looking a little deranged." She considered him with a long gaze, and he squirmed a little. "But, no, I don't think you're crazy. Just a bit lost, perhaps. Your dad told me a little about your mom and what happened. Who wouldn't feel lost after that?"

A bit lost. He turned the words over in his mind. Yes, that was an accurate description of the drifting of his mind or his heart or the *something* in him that he could not quite name but that always seemed to be wandering.

"How about those cookies, then?" Helena said, brushing her hands against each other as if dusting the serious conversation off of them. "Before my darling daughter turns into a chocolate chip herself because she's eaten that entire bowl."

Dee grinned widely, and her teeth were brown with evidence of her nibblings. "They're yummy."

"They'll be even better in cookies. Honestly, I don't know how you eat those things. They're semi-sweet, not even the full chocolate taste." Helena shook her head and turned back to the cookbook she had been perusing when the two children had entered the kitchen. "Peanut butter chocolate chip sound good you?" She glanced up at Nat.

"Yeah," he nodded. And, surprised at himself even as he continued, "That sounds really good."

The woman smiled, eyes warm behind her bright spectacles. "Good. That's good, hon."

Behind the stout woman, Dee crossed her eyes and stuck out her tongue at him in a broad display of what she called her rabid frog face, although Nat could never see anything remotely frog-like about it. It caught him by surprise and a laugh escaped him, just one, and more like a cough than anything else. But then another came, and another, and soon he was laughing so hard that his sides ached, that he he doubled over at the waist, so hard that tears leaked from his eyes. Helena rubbed his back as he hunched and shook in the cluttered kitchen, her hand a solid comfort against his heaving ribs.

"Cookies will be good for you," she murmured. "They always make things a little better."

———

That evening, Nat meandered through the gathering dusk with a ziplock baggie full of warm peanut butter chocolate chip cookies dangling from his fist. He breathed deeply, the scent of baking chocolate and peanut butter that still hung inside his nose mingling with the lush and dwindling warmth of the air, and he let it fill up his lungs, holding it in until his heart began to pound a protest and then he let it out in a slow, steady stream. The sound of crickets and the other chirping night insects flowed in symphony through his eardrums, a messy cadence that he let his sneakers try, mostly in vain, to keep time to as he walked.

He sighed, a deep heaving of contentment. Helena had been right, cookies did make things a little better. Opening the ziplock baggie and selecting a cookie, he took a bite, chewing as he walked, the chocolate chips still gooey against his tongue. With a swallow, he pulled another cookie from the bag and ate that one, too. Then he zipped the bag shut, planning to share the rest with his dad.

Helena had said, piling the freshly baked goodies into the bag just a little while ago, "Share these with that father of yours. And tell him not to be so afraid to trade a few words with me when we see each other. He's always welcome here, just like you."

Always welcome. He liked that. Nat didn't know if he'd ever been told that before, or if he'd simply felt it, even in his own home. *Always welcome.* Licking the crumbs from his lips, he hoped that they could make cookies again. His teachers at school were always saying that he was too skinny, that he was such a slip of a thing, that he needed to fill out a bit. *Cookies would help with that,* he thought with a quick grin flashed to the twilight. *Lots and lots of cookies.* His stomach churned and growled a little, and he couldn't tell if it was in longing or in protest. He had already consumed quite an impressive number of cookies before setting out for home.

The gray stones materializing out of the gloom, he cut a winding path through them towards the house. A couple of windows leaked a yellow glow, illuminating square patches of lawn, while the rest of the windows gaped dark and lifeless. Still smiling a little to himself, he took the steps up to the kitchen door in one big step, excited to share the cookies he had helped create with his father.

The man sat at the kitchen table, and looked up, face gray and haggard, as Nat stepped into the house. Nat stared at his father, the ease that had only just started to feel natural as it spread like butter over his skin freezing now.

"What is it?" he asked his father, feeling his own eyes grow large. "What's wrong?"

Don continued to stare for a moment, then blinked as if tunneling up out of a deep reverie. "You're back."

Goosebumps chased each other up and down Nat's arms, along his spine, and his heart began to beat faster. "Yeah," he nodded, "I'm back. But what happened? You look —"

"Where have you been?" His father's question cut across his own words.

"At Dee's house. We made cookies." He held up the bag of treats as evidence.

"At Dee's house," Don repeated.

The boy nodded. "I left a note. Want a cookie? They're peanut butter chocolate chip."

"I didn't know where you went," the man said as if he had not heard Nat. "I didn't see your note. I thought . . . I don't even know what I thought." He sighed. "I thought the worst, the absolute worst. You can't just wander off like that and not tell me where you're going."

Nat stared. "But . . . I always did before, and you never said anything. And I left a *note*." He stabbed a finger at the fridge, where he could see the scribbled-on paper still hanging.

"Yes, but you just said it — that was *before*. Before what happened. And now you tell me you were at Dee's house — *Dee's house*, where you could've — where the incident happened." Don shook his head. "That's unacceptable."

The boy felt his mouth twist into a tight scowl, a bolt of hot anger flashing across his stomach at the injustice. "Where I could've *what*, exactly?"

"Hurt someone. Or yourself."

Nat opened his mouth to argue, but shut it again, knowing there wasn't much he could say that he himself would believe.

"I worried all day, Nat, and I was just about to call the police. You need to tell me where you're going from now on."

"What if you're not around? You weren't even here today!"

"Then you come and find me, and if you don't find me you don't leave. Do you understand?"

Nat glared. Then, after a long pause, his fingers a tight fist around the ziplock baggie still dangling from his grip, he hissed through gritted teeth, "*Yes.*"

Don sighed, rubbed at his eyes. "Good. That's good." Another sigh. "Do you want any dinner?"

"No." Jaw still clenched, he plunked the bag of cookies down against the table, several of the cookies crumbling. "Those are for you. And Dee's mom says hello." He threw the words back over his shoulder as he stomped from the room, ignoring the prickle of guilt when he saw his father's eyes widen in surprise and hurt.

Good, he thought as he stormed up the stairs and into his room, slamming the door. *Good.* But, as he slumped onto the bed, he knew that he really didn't mean that, and he felt very secretly glad.

47

DON

Don woke in the gray dim just before sunrise the next morning with the awareness, the stark and utter knowledge, burning at the front of his brain. He had lost it, her journal. Somewhere, somehow in the last day he had misplaced the thing. And he knew, too, that he must find it. The need for it to be tucked away at the back of his dresser's draw stuffed with socks and underwear and squared handkerchiefs made him sit straight up in bed, eyes already blinking and squinting to shed a night's accumulation of crusty sleep. That it should be his first and most urgent order of business before anything else that day shone clear to the man, and he slid out of bed and began pulling on clothes without knowing what he donned.

The last place he remembered having the journal, feeling the soft and solid weight of its memory-laden pages, was in the cemetery. *I had it by her grave,* he knew, striding out of the house without even a cup of coffee, the screen door swooping open and then back into its place, uttering a stream of creaks and rattles. *When I went to visit her, I had it.*

The stones fell away on his right as he skirted their domain.
Sun rays began to glimmer at the eastern meeting of earth
and sky, but the prospect of stumbling his shins into granite
even in the dissipating darkness did not appeal to the grave-
keeper. So he strode around the residents, making for the
quiet seclusion of his family's plot. It occurred to him as he
strode through the dew-damped grass that one day it would
be his son walking along with another thirty or forty years of
time pressed in wrinkles into his forehead, going to visit
Don's grave, his corpse. *If he can forgive me*, the man thought,
clenching his jaw at the memory of his last exchange with
Nat the previous night, *If he can understand that parenting is
hard, and that I'm really no good at it*. The cookies had tasted
good, but left an ashy coating of guilt in his stomach, so he
had only eaten a few bites of one before setting the rest
aside.

He walked faster. Cookies and confections and confrontations
– he pushed all that aside. They could wait, they had to. Now
there was only the journal. Don remembered setting the little
book aside, laying it on the grass, buoyed up by the cropped
blades. *Maybe it's still there*. His stride lengthened, the tiny
collection of set apart markers materializing ahead. *Maybe.
Maybe maybe maybe*, chirped his brain in time with his feet.

And then he was there, the remains of his ancestors, both the
recently and the more distantly departed gathered beneath
the man's soles. Don scanned the ground, heart thumping
against his ribs. *It's here. Somewhere, I must have left it here.* He
circled around the granite stones, ducking his head low as he
looked. *It must be here.*

But it was not. There were no nooks or shrubs for the journal
to hide beneath, nothing to conceal it from view. If he had
left the book by his late wife's tombstone, it would be lying

in plain sight. And – his stomach felt as if it shriveled within his belly, tight and withered – it clearly was not. The ground spread bare around him in the warming light.

Gone, he thought, staring and then scowling at the offense of the unladen earth. *I've lost it.* Don shook his head at the audience of granite. *No. Not lost. Misplaced, for now. I'll find it.* Closing his eyes, he tried to envision what he had done after visiting with his wife, what unconscious thing he had done with her words. Nothing came.

The man turned and made for the house. He had brought it back there, then. It was the only logical option to his mind. The thing simply could not be anywhere else. Don told himself that again and again as the first fraction of the sun's disc slipped above the horizon. It would be there. He would find it.

4 8

NAT

Nat's first thought before he opened his eyes was that he was back in the hospital, his legs sore and tight at the end of the bed. He groaned and did not try to roll against the restraints that bound his ankles and wrists.

Stupid hospital, he thought. *I want to leave. I want to go home.*

Memories filtered through his awakening mind, recollections of Scrabble matches against his father stretching into the night, of his mother, years ago, humming along with the vacuum cleaner as she worked away in the living room, of the quiet of the cemetery in the afternoons, of Dee with her camera, and —

His eyes snapped open and the world swung about him as if he lay on a tire swing. He swallowed against the sudden nausea in his belly that had already launched bile up his esophagus. Down and down he forced it while his eyes, wide and fluttering along with his chest, took in the walls that were not teal, the bed without its monitor, the blue jeans he had fallen asleep in the previous night, chafing against his

skin through hours of dreamless slumber until they felt
bound and beaten by thick ropes instead of the worn fabric.

The hospital, the hospital, his brain sounded. Nat shook his
head, feeling his hair tug against the pillow. *No, not there, I'm
at home, I came home already. Not the hospital. Home.* He clung
tight to the word, the idea of the graves outside, his father
somewhere in the house or on the grounds, his own bed
buoying him up. The boy did not blink but stared around
him, afraid that letting his eyelids fall shut for even a
moment would break this strange spell and he would come
to surrounded by the vague stench of human skin and sweat
and the whirring of monitors behind his head and a needle
leaking fluids into his blood.

A muffled thump from down the upstairs hallway thudded
into his brain, his palpitating heart, making the boy jump.
Then came another, and the banging did not sound particularly like anything he would hear in a hospital. Nat sat up,
back creaking, and listened. More deep knocking sounds and,
as he slid to the floor, he could feel their vibrations reverber-
ating through his stretch-out socks and up his shins into stiff
knees.

Making his way to the door, he poked his head out into the
corridor and listened for a moment, then followed the sound
to his father's bedroom. Standing in the man's doorway, Nat
felt his eyes widen once again, stretching against the crunchy
sleep still lingering at their corners, taking in the scene of
disarray.

The poster bed spread unmade, blankets tousled across its
surface and partially hidden under piles of socks and under-
shirts and slacks and handkerchiefs that still held the creases
of careful folding but had fallen open. Empty drawers from
the gaping bureau leaned against the mattress, waiting to

take their fabric charges back once again. Across the room from where Nat stood, the closet door stood open and the boy could just see his father's back crouching low, throwing shoes behind him as he dug through the closet's contents. Every so often a shoe would fly off on an errant trajectory and collide resoundingly with the wall.

"Um," the boy said, stepping toward his father, "Dad?"

Don continued to burrow into the closet, jumping to his feet and beginning to shove the colony of pressed shirts along the rod where they dangled, sleeves swinging wildly.

"Dad!" said Nat, louder this time.

The man jumped and uttered a startled cry, hoarse and dry. He turned, flushed face draining to white even as Nat watched.

"I didn't hear you come in," said the boy's father, and Nat could hear the breathlessness in his voice.

"Sorry." He glanced around at the mess that gathered in the normally well-ordered bedroom. "What are you doing?"

"Oh. Well. I'm just looking for something."

"For what?"

"You know. Nothing all that important. Just one of those things."

"One of *what* things?" Nat frowned.

"Um. A book. I was reading a book, and I misplaced it." The man cleared his throat, coughing a little. "It was a good one and I wanted to finish it today."

"You put books in your sock drawer?"

Don swallowed. "Just trying to be thorough. And the place could use a good cleaning, so I thought I'd combine tasks. Be more efficient that way."

"Okay." Nat shrugged, but he could not push away the curiosity now flowing through him. *I wonder what book it is, if there is even a book at all.* If it was a good enough read to make his father throw his bedroom into chaos, the boy wanted to read it himself. "Can I help?"

"No!" Don spoke too quickly to add any truth to his words, and he knew it for a red blush blossomed over his forehead and down his neck. "No, I'll be fine. Thanks, though. You should go out, enjoy the day."

"Uh," said Nat, "okay."

The man nodded. A pause. "Did I wake you?"

Nat shrugged again. "I don't know. Maybe. It's okay, though."

Don's eyes narrowed a little as his muscles began to unwind. "Isn't that what you were wearing last night?"

This time it was the boy's turn to swallow hard. "I fell asleep in my clothes."

"Apparently. How are you feeling?"

"Just a little sore this morning, but fine, I guess."

Silence stretched across the room between the two, and Nat remembered how the steps had felt beneath his sneakers as he had stamped up them the previous night, tossing angry words at his father.

"Thank you for the cookies." Don's voice drifted over the mess, quieter than before. "They tasted very good."

"You're welcome." The boy picked up a sock and stretched it long for a moment before tossing it back down onto the bed. "Sorry I yelled at you. And that I didn't tell you I was going to Dee's house."

His father nodded. "We just have to be more careful, okay? I want to know that you're safe."

And that other people are safe from me, Nat thought, but he just nodded.

"Are you hungry? Can I make you some breakfast, pancakes maybe?" asked Don.

Nat shook his head. "No, I'm okay." *Pancakes are for Sundays.* "I'll just grab some cereal."

"I don't mind making them." A little smile picked at the corner of Don's mouth.

"I know." The boy thought he saw a flicker of remorse, even of guilt not connected to his father's search for the mysterious book. "Thanks, Dad."

The man dipped his head in acceptance. "Just let me know if you change your mind."

"Okay." Nat turned, but his father spoke again.

"Nat? We have to talk sometime about what happened, and what we're going to do next. Soon."

The boy swallowed hard, but when he met his father's eyes they were soft. "Yeah."

"How about tonight, at dinner?"

"Sure." Nat shrugged, not sure he really had any say in the matter.

"Just stick around the cemetery today, okay?"

Nat nodded and turned, and as he made his way down the stairs to the kitchen, he could hear his father begin to rustle and dig once again. *I wish I knew what book he's after.* He would tell Dee about it when he saw her, he decided as he began to pour himself a bowl of corn flakes.

MIA'S JOURNAL

I dreamed of a child last night, a tiny infant boy with the most perfect almond-shaped eyes, the down tuft of hair curlicuing across his fore-head soft enough to melt my heart. I woke with tears of love in my eyes and an ache pulsing somewhere deep within.

The whole thing reminds me of some Better Homes Christmas story of nostalgia and family and new life against all odds, the second rate writer determined to thread her tale with meaning but only succeeding in making it sickly sweet. Those stories always make me grit my teeth, against the sappiness they bleed and the putrid perfume samples tucked into the pages around each piece.

This dream of mine, even while it is cut from the same mold as those would-be tales of good feeling now that I push it to paper, it feels different. To me, at the very least, and isn't that what matters most? I hope, I hope, it makes me hope for something I cannot pinpoint. But it is enough, enough for now that I can kindle any hope at all in this long-cold brazier between my ribs.

It is the first dream of a child since she died. Since I banished my daughter from this life. The first of such a dream where my tears did not flow bitter and burning against my face, but warm as bubbles warmed by the sun in spring as they lift to the sky.

Hope. I can barely write the word.

What would Don think of it, of me? I don't feel worthy of such a luxury. I don't deserve the reprieve, or whatever this is.

I can still feel his new-birthed fingers curl around my own large one, the baby's fist pink and soft with fat. My son.

My son.

5 0

NAT

She waited in the tree, the one where she'd taken his picture, early sun melting through the boughs across her pink-painted cheeks. *Is this what I looked like to her?* Nat wondered as he gazed up at her, at her eyes closed in thought or reverie or even a delicately balanced, thinking back to when she had captured him with her Polaroid as he swung his knees in a different treetop and wrote.

This tree arched willowy and young over his mother's grave, over the collected remains of his family nestling close around. He brushed his fingers over the rough hewn top of the woman's marker, still cool from the night, the yellow roses blooming a heavy musk. The memory of the day he had watched her mahogany bed sink into the rectangular earth fissure crowded in close, and he shook and pushed it away and called up to his friend.

"Hey." His voice hung in the air.

Dee breathed in, long and deep, back arching to the sky as her brown eyes slid open. With a careful and somehow languorous stretch of her legs, bare feet flexing and then pointing like a ballet dancer, she smiled down at the boy.

"Hi yourself."

"Don't you have school?"

"Don't you?" she shot back.

"Dad said I could take some time off," Nat shrugged.

"That's what my mom said, too."

"What are you doing?"

"Lucy told me that she needed some exercise." He now noticed the camera secured about her neck, resting on the girl's belly, and a cornflower blue book clasped in one hand.

"Exercise, huh?" He rested a palm against the rough bark of the tree.

"Well, and she felt kind of bored." Dee patted the black shape with her free hand. "And I wanted to see you?"

Nat blushed at the revelation. "Get any good pictures?"

Tucking the book into an armpit and swinging the camera so that the strap hung diagonally across her chest, the girl clambered to the ground, sun dress and copper locks dancing about her able form. With a little grunt, she jumped the last stretch to the grass.

"Just some okay ones," she said, pushing her hair back from her eyes, tucking the curls behind her ears. "But I forgot that the light would be so dark."

Nat raised his eyebrows at his friend, then at the sky that was quickly turning overbright. "Dark? How early were you here?"

"Oh, I don't know," she said in just such a way that told Nat that she knew exactly when but didn't want to admit it. "Early. Before the sun came up."

He shook his head, "You're crazy."

"Maybe." She stuck her tongue out at him. "But you're the one hanging out with me. What does that make you?"

"Definitely crazier." He grinned back.

Dee bit her lip. "I don't mean that you're actually crazy, you know. Like, mentally unwell."

"Are you sure I'm not?" Nat said slowly, testing each word carefully. "I mean, *I'm* not sure I'm not."

"You're grieving. It's normal."

"I don't know how normal it is."

"The doctor said that you have complicated grief."

"They did?" Then, frowning, he continued, "How do you know what my doctor said?"

"Your dad told my mom." This time it was Dee's turn to shrug.

"Oh." Nat hadn't realized that their parents had been in contact. He supposed it was good that the two adults were.

With a smooth motion she raised the camera and snapped a photo before the smile had a chance to fade at all. "Gotcha!"

He snatched the developing square from the camera and laughed, grateful for the diversion. "Thanks."

The girl curtsied. "My pleasure." She craned her neck to see the resolving image. "You can keep it, I just want to see."

He dropped his eyes, watching his own features emerge as if rising up out of a bog, eyes and nose and lips topped by the indistinct mess of hair. And then came the details, the fractional separations between each tooth, the wrinkle of his forehead, the appling of his cheeks, twin mounds raised in mirth.

"Not bad," Dee said with a nod. "Considering what I had to work with." She poked him in the arm with a long finger.

Swatting at her hand, now Nat stuck out his tongue. "Very nice."

"I think so. generous, even."

"Yeah, yeah." He pointed at the book still tucked under her arm. Now he could see that its cover was lined in fabric "What's that? Are you writing now, too?"

Dee's smile dropped and lines of worry tracked across her forehead. "Oh. It's a book. I found it."

"Well, I can see that. I'm not that stupid." He gave a little half-smile, trying to ignore the knot of worry that his stomach had suddenly begun to curl into at the look on his friend's face. "What's it about?"

"It's a journal. So . . . it's about life."

"Anyone we know?"

She swallowed. "Sort of. I guess."

"Okay." Nat frowned at her. "Can you at least tell me where you found it?"

The creases on her forehead deepened. "Here." The word rasped up from her throat, dry and rattling.

"Here? You mean, in the cemetery?"

The girl nodded.

That didn't make much sense to Nat. Who would leave a journal in the graveyard? It certainly did not belong to him — that's what his spiral notebook was for, after all — and he didn't think his dad kept one. And he couldn't recall any visitors to the cemetery in the last few days, although he knew that he could be wrong, that he wasn't around all the time so someone could have come, could have planted some flowers and written to themselves, to their dead in the blue book —

And it hit him, the answer, with such force that he gasped. His father had been searching, ransacking his room for a book. And now, Dee had found one, here in the cemetery. Somehow, Nat knew that this was not just a journal his father kept, that it meant something so much more to make the man throw his room into such disarray with such zeal.

"Can I see it?"

She had the journal in her hands now, and her knuckles turned white around its pages. "Why?"

"Because."

"I found it."

"Here. In my family's cemetery."

"I'm not done reading it."

"Well, I'll give it back. I just want to see." He held out an upturned palm. "Please, Nat . . ." Her voice trailed away, as if she was not sure of what she wanted to ask.

"Look, I think it might be my dad's," he said, shrugging his shoulders. "He said that he lost a book. Maybe that's it."

"Oh." She glanced down at the cornflower fabric. "It probably is."

"I can give it to him." His hand still hovered between them, waiting. He began to tremble a little, the vibration beginning deep in his core and emanating out and out so that he wondered if the girl could feel it.

"Nat," she shook her head and sighed, eyes full of worry as she looked at him, "this journal . . . I think it belonged to your mother."

He swallowed and felt the blood empty from his face and neck, and he grew cold even in the warmth of the sun's light. "Oh," he said, and now his voice came faint and weak. "Oh." He swayed a little where he stood, and his hand sank back to rest at his side of its own accord.

"Are you okay?" she asked after a long moment.

Nat thought, forcing his mind to take stock of itself, of all of him. "I don't know." Another pause. "What's in it?"

"The journal?"

He nodded. "Yeah. The journal."

"I didn't finish reading it."

"But you did read it?"

She nodded.

He forced himself to accept the fact, to press on. "What did you read about? What did she say?"

"Different things. . . ."

"Like what?"

The girl sighed, shaking her head. "I don't know. I don't really get some of it, and a lot of it is pretty intense stuff."

"Intense?" Nat frowned. "What do you mean? Intense how, exactly?"

"Well, I think she was sick. She writes about that a lot."

"Sick? With what?"

"Look, maybe you should talk to your dad about this," said Dee. "I'm sure he knows more than the journal talks about, and he would definitely know more than me."

"Yeah, but . . ."

"But what?"

"I didn't know that my mom was sick. And Dad never told me anything about it. So . . . it might be weird to ask him about it, especially out of nowhere like this."

"It's not *that* out of the blue, not since I found the journal. I mean, if he knew you had it, he might expect to have questions. I know I would."

"You're not him, though."

She shrugged. "True. But neither are you, and you've got questions. Good ones, I think. So you're going to have to talk with him to get answers."

"I guess."

"Did he like the cookies?"

Nat blinked at his friend. "What?" His brain struggled to comprehend the question, to follow the jump in conversation topics, to tear his eyes away from the blue journal. *My mother's journal*, he thought. *She wrote in that, with her own hand.* He wanted the book, wanted to run his hands over the fabric, to touch what his mother had touched, to read words in her penned script. It seemed odd that he'd never seen her write in it when she was alive. She must have kept it to herself, like he did with his notebook. The idea filled his chest with a honeyed warmth.

"The cookies we made yesterday. Peanut butter chocolate chip, remember? Did your dad like them?"

"Oh." *Focus*, he told himself. *Cookies. Dad.* "Yeah. He said he liked them. I did, too."

"Good. My mom liked hanging out with you, by the way. She said to remind you to come by whenever you can."

"Sure. Of course." Nat could hear the distance in his own voice, but could not quite bring himself to care. All that mattered was the journal.

"We could go there now."

"Now?" *She knows*, he thought. *Dee knows what I want, and she's not going to give it to me.*

"My dad's starting a new painting project today, and we could watch and do some of our own painting. Or we could help my mom. She's going to work in the garden, start getting it ready for the colder weather."

"Cold?" This time Nat managed to muster some actual feeling for his words and interest in her reply.

"It'll start getting frosty soon enough, even in the early fall," explained Dee. "My mom doesn't want any of her plants to get caught in that without being ready. Especially the pumpkins. She's crazy about her pumpkins."

"Oh."

The girl sighed, blowing at the wisps of red hair that had fallen across her forehead. "I know that you want to read this, Nat," she said, ducking her head at the journal. "But I don't think you should. Not without your dad."

"Oh," he said again, looking between the blue bound pages and his friend's brown eyes. "Okay."

"I can't keep it myself, though. It wouldn't be right."

He waited, afraid to speak, afraid that he would not be able to keep the excitement that bubbled up in his lungs from leaking into his words.

"So you've got to promise me. Promise me that you won't look at this by yourself. That you'll only read it with your dad around. Promise."

Nat thought for a moment, then nodded. "I promise," he said, and he managed to keep his voice steady and solemn even while he twined his index and middle fingers about each other. He pretended that the motion made the lie okay.

She stared at him for what felt to Nat like a vast stretch of time. Slowly, slowly, she reached out both hands, the journal balanced between their twin paleness, and she trembled a little as she gave up the prize. And then the book was in Nat's own hands, the fabric soft and strong at the same time and he almost grinned, almost crowed in triumph as his heart danced inside his chest.

My mother's book, he thought, *and it's all mine!* He couldn't wait to open its pages, open a passage into her heart and life and mind, to know her better than he had in life.

"Thank you," he said, and his voice cracked a little.

Dee frowned, then nodded. "Don't forget," she said. "You promised."

"I know." He crossed his fingers again, just to be sure that the covenant would not bind him. "I know I did."

Her frown grew deeper, and her brown eyes seemed dark against her translucent skin, and even the peppering of freckles across her cheeks seemed to seep worry. But Nat could not bring himself to care much, and he ignored the twisting of guilt in his gut. A little dishonesty was worth it, he reasoned, for the prize he had won.

"I'd better go show this to my dad," he said finally. "He was looking for it, I think."

The girl nodded. "Okay."

"See you," he said, and he headed for the house at a lope, leaving his friend standing alone among the graves and the hedges thick with yellow roses.

51

DON

Don sat on the edge of the desk in his office, heavy with fatigue and despair. The floor, the desktop, the seats of every chair lay buried beneath strewn books and scattered stacks of paperwork and folders and stationary. He had upturned every drawer in his bedroom, the house, the cemetery office, emptied every space and spider-peopled corner, but there had been no sign of the cornflower covered journal. He sighed, and then the heaving breath turned without warning into a choking sob, and he sat in the midst of chaos and wept.

52

MIA'S JOURNAL

This bathroom smells of vomit. I have been sick all morning and can't imagine what is wrong as I sit here and shiver on the edge of the bathtub, waiting. Every time I move to leave, another wave of sickness washes over and over me and throws me face-first toward the toilet bowl once again, retching and dripping last night's dinner and the tea Don brewed for me this morning before he left me for the business of the dead. Although now there is not much left for me to offer that porcelain beast except a few paltry ounces of saliva turned to bile in my traitorous stomach.

My first vomiting since before the hospital, since I last stuck my finger down my throat and forced this body to operate on oxygen and caffeine and shreds of iceberg lettuce. I don't know what to make of that, what to think of myself and the then-me and the now-me and this bathroom rank with the scent of my reversed excretions. I can taste it between my teeth and I'm not sure if I actually taste the bile or simply can't imagine not tasting it.

It feels good to be so utterly empty, so drained. As perverse as the thinking is — disordered, I remind myself — I can't deny the feeling. I should drink something, but even water turns me. Even ice cubes. I feel the bile rising in protest. Swallow and gulp it down. Better the bitter than the bloating. Yes, better the bitter.

It comes again, very soon. I must succumb now. Into the fray I slide.

53

NAT

The boy lay on his bed, staring up at the ceiling. He felt as if he was one of Dee's mother's pumpkins, harvested and cut open and dug and dug and dug at until everything that had once been inside of him lay as a stringy mass of ooze and fiber at the bottom of a trash can and the space inside his rib cage yawned empty and cavernous and dead.

His mother's journal lay face down across his stomach, marking the place where he had stopped reading. He could not bear the words, pelting into him like a flurry of ice-sharp hail or fists or steel cased bullets — the poet in him could not decide which metaphor he preferred — the implication of their weight too much for his thin frame. He had needed a rest, a moment away from her scribbled pain. Although he did not know if it was the hurt she felt or what she inflicted on him now, years after the words' birth, that was the worst.

It felt strange to read of his father by name, for the man not to simply be "Dad."

Maybe Dee was right, his limp brain suggested. *Maybe I need him in this.* But Nat felt sure that his father would not allow him to keep the journal, and something inside of him needed to see the ordeal through to its gray and churning end, even if its only purpose was to see what he could take and still stand, still be Nat.

But it would be hard.

The boy licked his pale lips, picked up the book, and read: ". . . I wish to be rid of this second life. I never asked for it. . . ."

He put the book down, chest tight.

Did she really think that about me? He thought of the pumpkin waffles she had used to make just for him, dripping special designs in syrup over their basket tops, of how she read to him before she pulled the bed covers up to his chin and kissed him *good night, love*, and he felt the world tilt and spin about him. He clutched at a fistful of blanket and held tight as his eyes traveled back to the words and let them flow into him, cold as February rain.

54

MIA'S JOURNAL

life blood

flow between

beneath, deep

inside the rubescent

trail, slitted

passage, canal

of sex pleasure

pain and birth

all one

dichotic crimson

my blood is

yours his ours

i am earth

i am moon

pale and full

breasts swing

in the night pulse

sex and life

new sweat

births a child

———

i am full tonight

55

DON

Don watched the spaghetti percolate in the boiling water. Leaning over the pot, he closed his eyes as the steam rolled up over his cheeks, his lids, his forehead, enjoying how it scalded the skin there. The man ground his teeth together as the pain permeated deeper and deeper until he could no longer stand it and pulled away. He breathed in and in, the kitchen air now flowing cool and crisp through his airway. Shivering a little, the base of his back pulled and he felt old.

He had spent the late hours of the afternoon sitting by his late wife's grave, watching the bright noon sky fade into a deep blue streaked with the firebrand of sunset. That morning's desperate search had left him limp and emptied, and he wanted nothing more than to lay there in the cool grass until his breath ran out and he could join his ancestors, his charges, and — most of all — his wife in the earth. But as the sun traded places with the slivery moon, the great celestial changing of the guard, the tumult of the ransacking business pressed heavier and heavier against him until its weight drove him to his feet and into the office, the house, the bedroom where he set things back in their places.

Even so, still he did not feel quite right, and even the pasta's gentle flow and flux in the pot, the mesmerizing tangle that usually massaged into his brain, did nothing to ease the loss of the journal.

Stupid, he told himself, *Stupid and careless. How could you let her go so easily? I feel — I feel —*

But he pushed the thought away, resisted recognizing it, knowing it even as his heart beat with the fullness of its truth. That in losing the journal, he had somehow lost her again, and that it was worse than the first death because this time, this time it was his fault. Before, he had tried to pull her back from the brink of skeletal death, had fawned over her with caresses and specially cooked meals and doctors and therapists and love and love, the love in his heart, and he had failed but at least — at least he had tried, he had rallied, gathered the wagons and the cavalry and all the rest of those, he thought, ridiculous metaphors and put up his knuckles and *fought.*

This time, he was the killer, the disease. She had been dead, but now she was gone, truly and completely. The last scrap of her essence that he could hold to in the cold hours of the night when the bed stretched empty about him, when her words, twisted and full of wrong thinking as they were, bound her to him and he to her and he did not feel quite so alone.

A small voice murmured at the edge of consciousness, the far reaches of his reasonability. *Maybe this is better,* it offered. *Maybe this is the way it needs to be, for you.* The man swallowed hard. He didn't want this way, he wanted *her*, even as he recognized the impossibility of that desire.

And for Nat, said the voice. *He needs a father who is whole and here. Not drifting with the dead.*

Nat. Don thought, tried to recall the last time he had seen his son. Squinting into the rising steam, he stirred at the pasta. That morning, in his own bedroom, that's where he had last traded words with the boy. He wondered where Nat was now, what he was doing. The boy would be back soon, for the dinner and the talk that Don had promised to have.

He tried to focus his mind on that, on how he would say what he needed to say. How he would tell his son that he'd be tutored at home until January at least, instead of returning to school, to give him more time to heal and breathe and grieve freely. How his doctor wanted them to ramp up their counseling visits — not just Nat, but Don, too, with some sessions for the both of them together, three times a week for Nat, once for Don. How the therapist would focus on helping both of them feel and express the grief they needed to feel and express, but in a way that healed instead of harmed.

Don didn't know if he was up for the task. In fact, he knew he wasn't. But he also knew that was why he was seeing the therapist — for help. And that it was okay to need a little help. Or a lot of help. The doctor had said that, too.

Don tightened his fist around the wooden spoon and tightened his jaw and he promised himself that he would try — to work with his grief instead of fear it, to help his son do the same, to be the man that Nat desperately needed him to be. Even if he failed, even if he could never be both the father and mother that the boy deserved, Don would give his best, saving this second rate wallowing for the unfeeling dead.

Nat would come wandering in soon, he knew, and the man suddenly stirred at the spaghetti swirls with greater vigor, willing it into limp tenderness to coincide with the boy's hungry arrival. His blood felt like it flowed with a flush of the same spicy cayenne zest that he'd sprinkled into the simmer tomato sauce, cupboards seemed to fly open around him of their own accord as he lay the table with bowls and shining forks, glasses sparkling full and clear and clean, all set over eggplant colored placemats sewn by her hand years ago. He prayed over the food with words and with the desperate yearning that filled him, round and warm and deep.

Dusk shadows stretched along the rows of graves outside, and the man waited behind the kitchen's steamy panes, feeling something like hope for the first time in a long while, even through the loss of the journal.

DON

Don did not hear the dull thud that resounded from upstairs at first. At least, he did not recognize the sound in the same instant that his brain captured its existence, cradling it close. Instead the muted noise trickled through layers of consciousness and neurons and along the wending, winding trail of synapses already crowded with plans of pasta and the future and the dead woman — *No,* he told himself, told her visage that materialized in his mind, *not her. Not you, tonight, dear, not right now. You're gone, and it's Nat and me now, that's all* — and spices and warmed tomatoes crushed together, so it was a long minute's journey before the sound filtered into his knowing.

He paused in the final stirring of the simmering spaghetti, listening for a second noise, a reprisal to sound above the quiet popping bubbling up from the stove. Nothing met his ears, and he almost resumed his cooking, but something shifted and prodded from behind his belly button and would not let him forget the sound. So the man rested the wooden spoon on the counter and, turning down the heat of the stove's burners, strode from the room and paused at the foot of the stairs, eardrums straining into the cooler quiet there.

"Nat?" he called up. Still nothing. He hadn't heard the boy come in, didn't think there was another live soul in the house, but even so, he supposed, it wouldn't hurt to check, to be sure.

"Nat, are you up here?" Don asked as he ascended the steps, wooden boards creaking a little beneath his soles. "It's just about dinnertime." The upstairs corridor spread dark and silent before him. "I made spaghetti." *Again*, he added silently, sardonically amused at his lack of originality.

It was just the tiniest thing, barely a sound, barely a whisper, a stirring of the air. And yet it existed, birthed into being as a tiny hiccough shimmering out from the crack beneath Nat's bedroom door along with the bare dim that the man knew emanated from the boy's little bedside lamp. He leaned his ear in close where the door met the molded frame, knocked two knuckles against the wooden spread.

"Nat?" He knocked again. "You in there, son?" *Tap tap tap*, his knocking echoing strange and hollow in the hall. "Did you hear me? It's dinnertime."

Another sound that was more a shifting of the air than actual noise, only it grated more as a groan this time. Don's hand dropped to the round brass knob, palm resting against its cool surface for a moment.

"I'm going to come in, okay?" Still no answer but silence, his own words heavy in the quiet. Drawing in a deep and steadying breath without quite knowing why, the man's fist tightened around the door knob and he swung the door in and open.

Something slid along the floor with a little hiss, pushed by the moving edge of the door. Don glanced down as he entered, and felt every nerve that stretched through him twist and tighten. The little blue journal seemed to wink up at him as if it knew how it's presence here made everything feel that much harder.

A sound from before him, from inside the small bedroom, made the man blink and lift his eyes. His son lay on the bed, curled into a tight ball and trembling against the rumpled covers.

"Nat?" He stepped forward, over the journal – *her words, her touch spread out beneath him* – to rest a hand on that shaking back. "Son?"

The boy jumped at the touch, then slowly, slowly began to unwind his coiled torso. He turned his streaming face up to his father, shaking his head from side to side.

"She was right," and Don thought he was talking about his mother. "She said I shouldn't read it alone, and she was right."

"Who, son? Who was right?" the man murmured, afraid to hear the boy's answer. He peered closely into his son's eyes, both surprised and relived to see that, in spite of the tears, they seemed steady and clear.

Nat blinked at his father. "Dee," he said, as if was perfectly obvious. "She found it," he stared across the room at the blue book where it still lay, "out in the cemetery, by Mom's grave. She was reading it."

"Dee read your mother's journal?"

The boy shrugged. "Some of it. She told me that it was really intense, that I shouldn't read it alone."

Smart girl, thought Don.

"But I didn't listen. She made me promise I would bring it right back to you, that we'd look at it together, but . . . I lied." Nat looked at his hands where they lay in his laps, palms turned up like an offering. "I lied to her, and I took the book and I read it, all by myself. And . . ."

His voice trailed away, and the two figures posed, still and silent, for vast minutes.

"Son?" Don squeezed Nat's shoulder. "Talk to me. Please?" He both could and could not imagine what the boy was feeling.

"Did she — did Mom really hate me that much? Enough to want me to – to be dead?" The words trembled only a little, but Don could tell what effort it took for the boy to keep his voice steady.

"What?" The question came loud and unbidden from him. And then the man realized – *he didn't finish reading the journal. He doesn't know how it all turned out.* "No. *No.* Nat. Absolutely not. She did not want you dead."

"But she tried to – get rid of me, before I was born –"

"No. She made some poor choices, but she *never* tried to do that to you." He paused. "To anyone."

Nat frowned. "What do you mean, to anyone?"

Don sighed, passed a hand across his face and sank down to the mattress, feeling it sag under his weight as he sat. "There was another child, before you. Your mother got pregnant, but we lost the baby."

Nat's eyes gleamed wide in his pale face. "Because of her. Because she tried to kill it."

Don't shook his head. "Sometimes I'm still not sure, but mostly I believe that she didn't. It's all very complicated. Your mother, she went through a troubled time. She hated herself, and that bled into everything else. She couldn't help it. We lost the baby – a little girl, you know – because your mother hurt herself. It really had nothing to do with the baby, and definitely not with you."

"Oh." The boy sat, still gazing at his hands. "What was wrong with her? With Mom, I mean?"

"She had an eating disorder."

Nat nodded as if he knew what that meant, and Don realized that the boy probably did. He was nearly twelve, after all, and he'd probably learned at least a little about these things in school.

Don continued, "She got better, mostly, after we lost the baby. Sometimes the eating disorder thoughts would come back a little, but the worst thing was that it took a toll on her body. She was never quite as strong after that, physically. It was her heart that gave out on her in the end. Nobody expected it. Not so young, anyway."

"Why didn't you tell me?"

The man shook his head. "I know I should have. But it seemed — I don't know. It felt too hard." He looked up to see Nat's eyes blazing into his.

"It was too hard for me, too. I thought she'd — she'd *killed* herself, Dad." The boy prodded a finger into the coverlet. "You should've told me," he added, more quietly.

Don stared, feeling as if every last bit of air had been sucked from his body and that he was left as a vacuum, invisible and devouring. "That's what you thought happened, this whole time?"

The boy nodded.

"I — Nat — wow." Don's tongue felt too thick, his brain too slow to find the right words, but he knew that he had to try. "I'm so sorry. So sorry. I was trying to protect you. And — I failed. I failed you, terribly."

Nat shrugged, then nodded again. "It's okay."

"No," said Don fiercely, surprising the boy. "It's not okay. I messed up. I got so lost in my grief that I couldn't see through to you, couldn't help you. I'm so sorry."

"Lost," said Nat, as if the word felt familiar. "I got lost in it all too, I think."

Don squeezed his son's shoulders, pulling the boy close and, amazingly, Nat let him, and even pressed in harder. "I won't make that same mistake again. We're going to take some time, you and I, to figure this out. More therapy, more often, for both of us, both individually and together. You'll get to do your schooling at home for the rest of the semester. What do you think about that?"

"You're — you're not going to send me away?" Nat sounded incredulous.

"Of course not. Why would I?"

"Because I'm — I was — because I'm kind of messed up." And then, as an afterthought, "Lost.

"No. No way. We're in this together, you hear me?" Don pulled away to stare Nat squarely in the eyes. The boy didn't look away.

"Yeah," said Nat. "I hear you."

"It's what your mom would have wanted. Hell, it's what *I* want."

Nat leaned in again, and Don wrapped both his arms around him.

After a moment, Nat spoke again, voice unsure. "Did you name her?"

Don swallowed, knowing what he meant. "The baby girl?"

"Yeah. Her."

"Deidra. We named her Deidra."

"She's buried near Mom, isn't she? With the rest of the family."

Nodding, the man blinked at the sudden tears that flooded his eyes, hot and salty. "Yes."

"I've seen her grave."

"I'd imagine that you have."

"But I never thought about it before." The boy paused. "It makes sense, I guess."

Don said nothing.

"Why did Mom hate herself?"

He sighed. "I wish I knew. Maybe if I could have figured that out, I could have saved her. Could have stopped her from dying, could've saved her from the voices inside her."

The quiet lengthened, grew deeper, more still. The man clasped his hands together as if in prayer. "Nat."

The boy looked up at him, meeting his eyes.

"I want you to understand something. Your mother was sick. More than any of us knew — you or me, even the doctors couldn't fix her or make her well or give her what she needed." He paused, trying to collect his swirling thoughts, to trade understanding with his son. "She was sick for a long time. Long before you came along."

"I know."

"It's not your fault. You didn't do anything to her to make her worse or hate you or force her to do the things she did. She was already like that, probably before I met her. I don't know what happened to her, what went on to make her brain work the way it did. I couldn't figure it out when she was still with us, and I can't now."

"I know, Dad."

"And," he drew a deep breath, "she loved you very much. As much as I do now."

Nat dropped his gaze back to his hands.

"She did. I promise. All those things that you read, the awful things that she wrote about your sister — she didn't feel like that with you. She had begun to change, to heal, and I think that loosing Deidra, as awful as that was, helped your mom with that. So when she became pregnant with you — she was so lovely, Nat, so full of joy. I can't even begin to tell you how much she wanted you, how happily she waited for you to be born. How much she adored being your mother and raising you and watching you grow so tall."

"Why?"

Don shook his head. "Because you were hers. You still are. She loved you, God, so much. If you keep reading her diary, and the ones that come after this, she begins to write about it, to talk about you."

"If she loved me so much, why did she let herself die?"

The man sighed again. "Because she was sick, like I said, and even though she had begun to get better, she had bad days where she would slide back into her old ways, where she would not eat or treat her body poorly. Habits are hard to break, and your mother's was probably nearly as old as she was. Her heart was already weak. It could only put up with so much. She fought for life, that's for sure." Don felt his voice grow stronger as the truth spilled out of him. "Some days she fought harder than others, but the important thing is that she fought. She didn't just let herself die. She didn't want that. She didn't want to leave us — to leave you."

Nat looked up at his father, forehead furrowed with tangled worry. "Are you telling the truth? Or are you lying to make me feel better?"

He smiled a little at the directness of the question even while his heart wilted at the hurt in the boy's heart that brought it into life. "I haven't lied to you, I swear." He glanced at the blue journal, still and silent across the floor. "Would you like to see for yourself? We can read more together, you and I. Like your friend suggested."

The boy followed his father's gaze, pursing his lips. "No," he said after a moment. "No, I don't want to read any more. I've heard all I want to, I think."

"That's okay. In fact, it's probably a good thing." *I don't know how much I could take, anyway*, he thought with some relief.

"Yeah. Probably," the boy echoed.

"Nat."

"Yeah, Dad?"

He stared down at his son, wanting to show him his mother's love, to express his own gut wrenching feeling for the child, but all words died in his throat. Instead he found himself pulling the boy close in a tight, fierce embrace, crushing Nat's head into his chest with such strength that he wondered that the boy did not pull away or protest. But Nat did none of these things, twining his own arms around his father's torso and squeezing until he shook with the effort.

The two figures sat, limbs and hearts and genes and drying tears entwined as the dusk deepened to night and the simmering pasta water cooled downstairs, forgotten in the empty kitchen.

NAT

Nat had never realized how deeply his mother wanted her skin to wrap tight about her bones, how desperately she had to fight the sickness inside her that wanted her to waste away into nothingness.

He remembered how she would only pick at miniature servings from her plate at dinner even while she piled his plate, and his father's plate, with whatever warm and wonderful dish she had bent over in preparation. How his father would frown and push at his own food, and later Nat could hear them arguing and he'd catch flashes of arguments, "the doctor said" and "don't forget" and "just let it go, please." The muffled fights would bleed into his sleep and he'd shiver through the night.

But always in the morning his mother would smile at him, at his father, and see them both off to their respective day's adventures with a swooping kiss and hug. His father would catch her up, sometimes, in a vast, enveloping hug and waltz her over the kitchen linoleum before taking his leave for the office, and Nat would laugh at the display and laugh in the knowing that all was well in this, his tiny corner of the world, safe and warm with the dead spread all around.

But that knowing had been wrong, or only a half-truth, perhaps. His mother wasn't the light-filled soul he'd always believed her to be, with words and with her feathery lips pressed hard and soft against his forehead at bedtime, with the way she smoothed his hair back when he sat on her lap and they read together, her voice weaving the story around and around the pair. No, she cared more for herself, for raising him as fast as time would allow so she could be rid of him, so she could live for *her*, the son a burden she could not wait to shed.

He sat up from where he lay on the bed, snapping the journal shut. The cornflower cover seemed to mock him in the yellow haze of the bedside lamp, laughing at how he had expected comfort, closeness with the woman who had never cared for him at all.

"I hate you," he told the book in an even voice. He listened to how the words felt sliding off his tongue, how they hung in the air and expanded to fill the bedroom's stillness. And again, but this time he ground them through clenched teeth. "I hate you."

He hoped she could hear him, wherever her disembodied soul now lived. For the first time in two years he found himself wondering if she really dwelt in heaven, and almost, *almost*, hoped that she did not, that she was in the other place.

She deserves it, probably, he thought, and then felt frightened and disgusted with himself at the notion, at his own horrible and traitorous mind. But the book still lay heavy in his hand, too cheerfully colored, too full of truths he did not wish to know, and the fright flashed into anger, hot and sick and heavy over his breastbone.

He flexed his arm and hurled the book across the bedroom, enjoying how the pages fluttered in brief flight before slamming with a satisfactory thud against the opposite war and then again down against the floorboards.

"I hate you." This time the words came thick as he uttered them through the suddenly blur and flush of tears. Twisting his body about over the wrinkled bedclothes, he rubbed his face against the comforting texture of his pillow and let the rising sobs crest up and out of him, their breaking loud and soft around him through the muffled cotton.

5 8

NAT

The boy found Dee standing in front of his mother's grave the next morning, her muscular form as she held a bouquet of daisies, the epitome of every cemetery visitor come to pay respects and shed requisite tears over some beloved remains or another.

"I brought flowers," she said as he approached.

"For her?" He nodded at the granite slab.

She shrugged. "I couldn't decide if I wanted to give them to you or to her. So . . . here." She thrust the bundle at him, and accepted the waxy stems.

"Thanks."

"You can do whatever you want with them." She paused, staring at him as if trying to read his thoughts. "Sorry if you don't like daisies."

"I like daisies fine." He lifted a corner of his mouth in a half smile. "You got flowers for a boy. Isn't it supposed to be the other way around?"

"Is it? That seems very old—fashioned of you." She raised her eyebrows. "Even if that's true, I don't really care all that much. Do you?"

He thought for a moment. "I guess not."

"Then it's settled."

"I read the journal." His admission came out of nowhere, even though he had known he would tell his friend what happened, had planned to.

"Oh?" She tried to feign indifference, and failed.

"You were right. It was . . . intense. I shouldn't have read it by myself."

"You read it alone?" Her eyes widened. "But I told you — you *promised* —"

"I know. I did. And I'm sorry. Sorry to you, and sorry that I didn't listen. Really, I am." He swallowed, wiped the palm of his free hand against his denim shorts. "You were right."

Dee crossed her arms. "Fine. I can believe you, I suppose. So . . . are you okay?"

He shook his head. "I don't really know." *Will I ever be okay? Could any of this be okay even after a thousand lifetimes?* The boy did not know the answer. "But I did talk with my dad about it. About her."

"Oh!" Her face lit up at this revelation. "Well, that's good."

"Yeah. We talked a bunch about her, and how sick she was. She nearly starved herself to death, you know."

"Yeah. I sort of picked that up," she admitted.

"And apparently I have a sister. Or had one." He shook his head, confused.

"I read about her. What happened was just . . . it sounded so awful."

He nodded. "Yeah. But . . . she didn't hate me like she hated Deidra. That was what they called my sister."

"I don't know if she even hated Deidra," Dee said. "I mean, maybe your mom said she did, but I don't think it was really true, deep down. If it was true, she wouldn't have been so sad when she lost the baby."

"Maybe." Nat shrugged. "All I know is that Dad told me that she began to get better after Deidra, and after me. And that her heart was weak, and that's what killed her in the end."

Dee leaned in, clasped his thin hand between her callous-smoothed palms. "I'm glad we're friends," she said.

The boy felt his brows lift in surprise. "Me, too," he said after a moment, and smiled at his friend, at how her berry pink lips twisted in concern, at how the sunshine caught in her copper hair.

He gazed down at the marker of his mother's tomb, very aware of the tiny stone of his dead sister's grave on the periphery of his vision. *It's strange,* he thought, *how much the dead can hurt people, even when they're gone and buried.* His dad would probably say that the dead still had a lot to teach the living.

"I bet she was a wonderful lady," Dee said, following his gaze. "I wish I could have known her."

The trees rustled as if in reply, and for one wild, beautiful moment Nat feels like his mother is close, and happy, and safe.

He smiled. "I wish you could have, too," said the boy, and meant it.

ALSO BY ELIZABETH WILDER

Night Cycles: Poetry for a Dark Night of the Soul

Balefire: Poetry for the End of the World

A FREE EBOOK FOR YOU

A SHORT **COMEDY**

THE
BOOK
OF
LAZARUS

ELIZABETH **WILDER**

CAN'T GET ENOUGH WILD(ER) WRITING?

Download *The Book of Lazarus,* an irreverent and intelligent short
comedy about one of history's most notorious miracles — totally
free!

Grab your free book here:

https://tinyurl.com/book-of-lazarus

ABOUT THE AUTHOR

Elizabeth Wilder writes, paints, and dreams in Montana. She is the author of two poetry collections: *Night Cycles*, poetry for the dark night of the soul, and *Balefire*, poetry for the end of the world. Her words and art have appeared in various publications, such as xoJane, Somerset Studio, Still Standing Magazine, Wild Goslings, and Disney's Family Fun.

In addition to her quirky little family and their too-many naughty — and very much loved — dogs and cats, Elizabeth is in love with moon-gazing, dancing wild, and drinking too much coffee.

www.sheofthewild.com